BEGIN
THE
WORLD
AGAIN

Inscribed for Carolyn Hall,
dear friend, role model, and
artist. Thanks for all your
Kindnesses!
love
Bettie Cannon
1996

BEGIN THE WORLD AGAIN

BETTIE CANNON

Charles Scribner's Sons • New York
Collier Macmillan Canada • Toronto
Maxwell Macmillan International Publishing Group
New York • Oxford • Singapore • Sydney

Charles Scribner's Sons Books for Young Readers
Macmillan Publishing Company
866 Third Avenue, New York, NY 10022

Collier Macmillan Canada, Inc.
1200 Eglinton Avenue East, Suite 200
Don Mills, Ontario M3C 3N1

First Edition   1 2 3 4 5 6 7 8 9 10
Printed in the United States of America

Library of Congress Cataloging-in-Publication Data
Cannon, Bettie Waddell.
Begin the world again/Bettie Cannon.—1st ed.
p.   cm.—(Charles Scribner's Sons books for young readers)
Summary: Feeling crowded and trapped in the farm commune where she has spent most of her life, fifteen-year-old Lake can find no hiding place from everything going wrong with the farm and with her parents.
ISBN 0-684-19292-6
[1. Communal living—Fiction.   2. Farm life—Fiction.
3. Parent and child—Fiction.]   I. Title.   II. Series.
PZ7.C17138BD   1991   [Fic]—dc20   90–46596

With love for Michael, Ned, Matthew, Sarah,
Jesse, John, Kate, and Mollie
who can . . .

ACKNOWLEDGMENTS

Although this is a novel and not a history, grateful acknowledgment is offered here to three generations of women whose experiences led me into this story, including: Candace Anderson, Michigan's singer/historian; Erin Driver and the memory of her grandmother, Eleanor; Zoe Neal and her grandmother, Barbara Neal, my lifelong friend. Acknowledgment is made also to Wendell Berry, whose books and poems about his beloved land inspired; to David Tresemer, whose book (*The Scythe Book*, Hand & Foot, Ltd., 1981) informed; to writers like Richard Goodwin (*Remembering America*, Little Brown, 1988), Kathleen Kinkade (*A Walden Two Experiment: The First Five Years of Twin Oaks Community*, Morrow, 1973), and Joan Baez (*And a Voice to Sing With*, Summit Books, 1987), who helped me remember "those times"; to Clare Costello for her understanding as editor and skill as teacher; to Ragdale Foundation, Lake Forest, Illinois, which gave me time and space to work; to my friends in Detroit Women Writers, who heartened me with their insight and encouragement.

1

It was a month or so before her sixteenth birthday when Lake saw Sun Dog for the first time. It was spring and just barely dusk when he came winding down the hill, past the barns, toward the Big House. From inside the screen door Lake watched him, and she braided and unbraided a strand of her long brown hair over and over. He came down the gravel lane through the aisle of barely green trees, moving as if he couldn't wait to get where he was going. The guitar slung across his back bobbed up and down and, like an outlaw in an old western, he wore a broad-brimmed black hat. Halfway down the lane he stopped, took it off, and wiped his forehead with his forearm.

His lean body tilted forward, his black hair bounced like a child's, and light from the low, late sun reflected from the buckle on his belt into her eyes.

He sang in a raspy, rough, and high-pitched voice—something about looking for a home.

When he hit the first step he rolled up his dusty black hat and stuck it into the waistband of his cutoff jeans, which were so short that the pocket linings hung down below the fringy edges. He wore thick leather moccasins, dusty and broken down at the heels. Now Lake could see a name engraved deeply, ornately on the square silver buckle at his waist. He stopped singing.

"This here reads 'Sun Dog,' Missy," he said.

He rubbed the inside of his wrist back and forth across the buckle. When he smiled, a wide gap showed between his big front teeth.

"A lady artist more 'n six feet tall gave me my name on a day when the halo around the sun was like a neon sign in the sky," he said. "Then out of the goodness of her heart she cast this for me. That was out in Colorado at the Cosmic Freedom Farm, if you know where and what that might be."

Lake did know about the Cosmic Freedom Farm, and she shuddered in remembrance, but the man kept talking.

"Sun Dog's the name. You in charge here?"

"No," Lake said.

She wanted to lock the screen, but there were no locks anywhere on Barataria Farm. Didn't he know this was a Kentucky farm community and not a Colorado commune and no one was "in charge"? Didn't he know everyone tried to be equal on a farm like Barataria?

She could repeat word for word what Tyler often said. "We're building a tribe here. It's our conscious commitment to learn to live together as equals. We do it by saving the land. That is our redemption."

Hadn't her parents and their friends been trying their best to live that way for fifteen years, ever since 1964?

"You aren't in charge?" The man paused, waited as if he were picking his teeth or listening for something no one else could hear. "Well, why not? Why in hell not, little green-eyed lady?"

2

No one had ever called her "little" before, or "green-eyed lady." For a minute she didn't know what to do with her hands, and her knees felt weak. He laughed in that high-pitched voice, and his laughter seemed to teeter on the edge of something dangerous.

"You can talk to Tyler Gillespie," Lake said. "He's inside."

She had done it again. Like everyone else, she called on her father when new people came or when town people caused trouble or when there was conflict in the family itself. She had lived all of her fifteen years on communal farms in three different states, and it was still hard for her to remember that here on Barataria Farm no one was in charge, or so the adults pretended. The man with his name on his belt twisted out of his backpack and leaned his guitar against the wall. He brushed his hair back from his face with both hands, combed his short, black beard with his fingers, opened the door, and came into the house. When he passed close by her in the hallway, she saw that he was younger than he seemed.

Almost every day in spring and summer newcomers showed up at Barataria Farm, grown men like Sun Dog, maybe sent by Ty's old friends or saying they'd read about the life Ty and his group were trying to live. Some newcomers were women not much older than Lake. They came down the narrow lane between the colonnade of oaks with babies slung across their backs or held in front for nursing. The strong women like Selene, Lake's mother, didn't like it when the girls arrived half sick and a little crazy. Some who came were runaways who thought they'd find freedom there. When the teenagers arrived, often strung out on drugs, Lake wanted to tell them a few things about freedom. They'd soon find out if they stayed. Tyler and Selene said the runaways' kind of freedom was a negative thing, going away from something, not toward something.

No, they weren't going to find their kind of freedom here. For one thing, drugs were out, taboo, forbidden. For another, children and teenagers and grown-ups were treated exactly alike.

"If you don't work, you don't eat. Easy when you know the rules," Ty said. "That's the way it is. Fair and equal."

Everyone agreed.

Lake tried not to mind about this stranger, this Sun Dog person coming right inside the house as if he owned it. Openness and sharing are the ideal, Ty and Selene believed. But why then did Lake sometimes yearn for space of her own with just her own parents? Why did she hate not having any clothes of her own or her own room the way Vernelle Fox and the other girls at school did? Why did she hate it when strangers came right in the front door as if they belonged there the same as she?

Sun Dog could have been Ty's age, thirty-six or thirty-seven, or he could have been much younger. She couldn't tell now. His brown eyes were intense, vague like those spiritual types who look deep inside you before you are ready to let them. She'd known plenty of people like that at the Cosmic Freedom Farm. Sun Dog crossed the hallway, walked toward the sounds coming from the dining room: sounds of children talking, laughing, horsing around, and Tyler's after-dinner-story-time voice rising above the others. Ty had memorized scraps of poetry when he was a boy, and he loved taking his turn to recite or tell stories to the children after dinner.

"If the clouds move off, you'll see the full moon tonight," he was saying, "and it'll be the second one to show its face this month. That's why we call it the 'blue moon,' even though it isn't blue at all. That's where we get the saying 'once in a blue moon.' You keep watching the sky, you'll see it."

Lake followed Sun Dog into the room. In one corner, with their farm journals, field maps, and planting charts spread out on the table, Free and some of the others were arguing about whether to buy another cow or not. They'd been arguing about it all winter. Without waiting for Lake to say something first, Sun Dog walked right in and told them who he was. Ty stood up, making little tents with his fingers against the table.

"I heard about you, man," Sun Dog said. "Let's see—the Whole Earth Catalog? Maybe one of those alternative culture newsletters?" he said, rubbing his beard. "Don't exactly remember which. I'm looking for a home with the right mix of purpose and people."

Nobody said anything.

"And I do hope," he went on, "you need a sower of seeds, a talker, a man of no ego? A man who has transcended all material connections?"

Ty took one step backward. Maybe he couldn't think of what to say any more than she could, Lake thought. Ty introduced Sun Dog to Andy, who had been with them from the beginning. Andy, along with Tyler, had driven the Volkswagen bus when they had searched across three states for the right farmland. Now Andy, the big red-bearded carpenter, waved a pan at Sun Dog in greeting. Soapsuds ran down his thick muscular arm.

"Andy burned the rice," Ty said, looking at Sun Dog. "Around here, you burn it, you clean it."

Next Ty pointed toward Andy's son.

"That's Kesey. He's fourteen."

5

"He named for who I think he's named for?"

Sun Dog was right, Lake thought. Kesey's mother, who left long ago, named him for Ken Kesey, whose travels with his Merry Pranksters in their crazy-colored bus influenced Selene and Tyler's whole generation. Kesey, as he always did, watched Andy, put both hands in his pockets the way Andy did, and didn't look up.

"That's Lake who brought you in," Ty continued. "You'll meet the others out in the barn. Most of us sleep out there. Maybe if you stay long enough, you'll get a little space of your own. Oh yeah. And, uh, Sun Dog? Everybody works here. You need to know that."

Ty gave his regular newcomer's speech. "Tomorrow you'll sign up for a job. You'll get to do what you want to do." He smiled and looked up over his eyebrows. "Most of the time, that is. New people usually cut brush their first time out. And we've got a lot of that to do before haying and corn planting overtake us."

"You wait and cut that hay in the old of the moon," Sun Dog said. "It'll dry a lot faster."

There was a long pause. And then in a voice gone low and quiet Ty said, "We have meeting once or twice a week, or more if someone thinks we need it. We talk things over. We . . . You'll be on probation and then we vote . . ."

"Man," Sun Dog said, and grinned his gap-toothed grin, "could it be maybe I might have found me a home?"

Lake noticed the way he ignored Ty's voice, the small silence. He would learn, if he stayed, that Tyler didn't like it when newcomers told him what to do. Even Tyler didn't seem to know that about himself. But Lake did. She'd been studying her father for a long time, ever since she could remember.

Sun Dog clapped both hands onto Ty's shoulders and

6

drew him into an embrace. Tyler hesitated again, but only for a moment. Then he laughed, too, and hugged Sun Dog back. Then the rest of the family stood up, surrounded Tyler and Sun Dog, and hugged each other in a big clump of arms and faces and hair. Lake watched from a corner of the room.

Later Andy took Sun Dog down to the barn to look for a place to sleep, and Tyler went upstairs where Selene, Lake's mother, was busy with her weaving. Tired of waiting for the blue moon to show itself on that cloudy April night, the younger children dropped off to sleep one by one in corners of the community room across the hall, entwined together like puppies.

After she filled the lamps with oil and trimmed the wicks smooth, Lake followed the others across the yard toward her sleeping place in the Children's House, the small bungalow where Ty, Selene, and Andy had lived first when they came to Barataria in 1974. When they had finished renovating the Big House, building the office, two community rooms, and more eating space, the small house was given to the children to live in and decorate exactly the way they wanted. Lake thought it sounded a lot better than it was in real life. The little kids didn't care if the tiny house was clean or even neat. There was no real furniture, only pillows and sleeping bags. In all four rooms there were weird constructions of rocks and twigs, cages for baby rabbits and snakes and who knew what else. Lake hated looking at the wild, complicated pictures drawn on the walls as if they were someone's nightmare and no one had come to comfort the artist-dreamer.

When Lake complained at meeting about the smell and the mess, the adults said, "We feel that you guys can figure

7

it out. Just think. Think for yourselves," they said. "It's best if you do it yourselves. You're full members of this community."

It turned out that even the littlest child had different ideas about how the house should be, and the children argued about everything just like the adults, only longer and louder. Finally all Lake could do was leave signs in her own little corner upstairs in the loftlike room to protect her space.

THIS SHELF FOR MY ROCK COLLECTION ONLY!
KEEP OFF.
LAKE'S BED ONLY!

Lake felt her way through the dark house and up the steep, narrow stairs. There was a sleeping child in her bedroll, so she carried her, bed and all, to an empty corner. The only sleeping bag she could find for herself smelled like urine and there was sand in it. As Lake shook it out she wondered why no one understood that the space in the upstairs loft with its windows overlooking the hay fields was hers. The children's reasons for getting into her territory weren't thought out like Ty and Selene's reasons, but it all meant the same: Lake didn't have a place she could call her own.

From her windows she saw the moon rise above the dark shapes of trees in the wood lot at the field's edge. She thought about the sleeping children who had waited so long to see Ty's blue moon, how it had outlasted them. She stared at the perfection of the moon and the long shadows it cast across the yard. Maybe, Lake thought, maybe I ought to wake the little kids. But before she made up her mind someone, a man, walked out of the barn into the yard. Stretching his arms high over his head, he turned a perfect cartwheel across the open, moonlit yard. She pulled the curtain back. It was Sun Dog. His long hair falling over his face, he turned another cartwheel. Then as he wheeled over and over down the hill in the moonlight, Lake heard his raspy, high-pitched voice singing, "... *without a home* ..."

Singing, shouting the old song, he disappeared into the trees and over the low riverbank. The singing stopped. The moon shone down, pouring its light over the fan of water sprayed out by Sun Dog's body as it plunged into the river. Like spent fireworks, the sparkling water swung there in the light and then fell back to Earth. Into that silence came Sun Dog's cry, and he sang again, "*without a home* ..."

2

As Lake pulled a T-shirt over her head, she decided to find Selene, tell her about Sun Dog's arrival, about her dream. She had slept fitfully, dreaming about water and cartwheels and James Dean. Why would she dream about a dead movie star she didn't know? Vernelle Fox, her best friend at school, had a poster of him, but Lake didn't even like him, dead or alive. Somehow he seemed menacing.

The familiar mists still floated above the fields as Lake went outside. She knew where Selene would be. Selene was in the same place a lot these days. Lake headed for the chicken coop, the old chicken coop made into the washhouse.

She held her breath, putting off the moment she'd have to breathe in the smell of old straw soaked with chicken droppings, which still clung to the low, whitewashed building. She wrinkled her nose as she ducked under the clothesline hung with sheets and towels, and went inside. There were clothes inside, too, hung on lines stretched across the room where roosters once crowed and hens laid their eggs. This was the washhouse and what the family called the "clothes closet." As usual, Selene was there doing whatever it was she did these days.

"So here you are," Lake said, exhaling. "Are you hiding out down here?"

"You think I am?" Selene's voice was flat as she smoothed out a towel on the long table. Staring out the window, she folded the towel without looking at it.

Lake sat on the table swinging her legs back and forth. "I'm . . . I don't know, worried about you. Even when you're here, you're not here. You just say 'yes,' 'no,' 'maybe,'" Lake said. She wondered what had happened to the Selene who spoke up at town council meetings, talked about recycling glass bottles and newspapers. "This isn't the Selene who bullied everyone into digging a new garden and made them finish it in a week. Now is it? Are you okay? Really, I mean it."

It was as if this new Selene were living by rote, not in the right now.

"I'm okay," Selene said. "I'm just, you know, a little down. Besides, look at this wash. Laundry is like grass. It grows, you mow it, and it grows again." Selene pressed a no-color, ragged towel with the flat of her hand, stacked it on top of the pile, and pressed it all down with both hands.

"Well, I guess you're here because you like it, Selene," Lake said. "You sign up to do the wash because, even if it does stink down here, you like this place."

It was true. The washhouse in the grove of ash trees close to the river, with its low ceilings and small, confined space, didn't swallow Selene up the way the rooms in the Big House seemed to do. Those rooms were high-ceilinged and square, with tall, narrow windows that didn't fit Selene's smallness. The Big House was messy and noisy,

11

confusing, while the washhouse was plain and quiet, furnished with three metal tubs, a long, porcelain-topped table, and a wood stove. In one corner there was an old Easy Spin-Dry washing machine that Free Adams had found in a yard sale and which Andy had repaired. Shelves built around the room held clean sheets, towels, shirts, and jeans, clothes enough to outfit everyone in the commune. That meant sometimes fifteen people and sometimes twenty or more.

"Where were you last night? Did you eat?" Lake said.

"Nope. I got going on the loom and . . ."

"I wish you would eat, Mom. Selene."

"Don't call me Mom," Selene said.

It was part of Selene's belief that they all were one family; everybody belonged to everybody else and to no one.

"Yeah. Right. I know," Lake said. "Children are equals here. I don't belong to you and Ty. You know how that makes me feel, Selene."

"Lake, let me tell you, you're far better off. You and Kesey and the rest of the kids are learning all kinds of talents and strengths from a lot of different people, not just two tired parents," Selene said.

The women on the farm were always talking about how much they'd been damaged growing up in a nuclear family.

"It ends up that we have to do what everybody says, not just you. It's always Andy who decides. He might as well be the only parent we all have. He's the most . . ." Lake couldn't think of what it was that Andy was.

"He's the most conservative, right?" Selene finished for her.

"Mom!" Lake said it again without thinking. Selene

didn't answer to "Mom" or to "Eliza," either. Eliza was her old name, her name from the other world back in the sixties, the famous sixties everyone talked and wrote about all the time, the time of the Vietnam war, the student protesters. That's where Selene met Tyler Gillespie IV at a protest march in California. Two idealists on their long march toward the right way to live, as Tyler always said. So Eliza became Selene, the moon woman. With a few stops along the way, they finally got to a Colorado commune, the one Sun Dog had been in, too. The one where all the members had to be born anew and rearrange their families into one big group. It was the place Lake remembered with so much fear.

"It's getting nice out. Warm and . . ." Lake said, trying to cheer Selene. "You like working in the orchard, the garden . . ."

"That's why I hung the clothes outside today. In here they mildew before they dry." Selene folded another faded towel, stiff from drying in the hot windless air. "You sound like Lana, always wanting me to do something different from what I am doing."

Lana was in charge of the work list and always knew who was doing what. Because Lana liked driving the tractor and pulling stumps out of fields every chance she got, she could spot "men's work" or "women's work" discrimination a mile off. Housework was listed in her book as "unpleasant duty" and not just for the women to do. She gave you extra time-off credits if you chose washing dishes or laundry or cooking as your job for the day. Even so, laundry and dishes didn't get washed, clothes didn't get mended, and dinner didn't get cooked unless those jobs were assigned. Some people, especially the newcomers, said at meeting that assigned work interfered with their freedom. But in the end most agreed that Lana was right. Everyone had to do some of the unpleasant work sometimes. They always worked it out with some combination of noisy confrontation and trust and love that Lake didn't understand. But she loved seeing it all happen.

Selene picked up her guitar by its worn macramé strap.

"This is what I do while the clothes wash. Just noodle around. All by my lonesome."

"I don't want to hear you talk about being lonesome," Lake said, jumping down from the table. "I need a clean shirt."

She flipped through a stack of shirts. "These are really ugly."

"Lake, come on. A shirt is a shirt. Just take one. Smell it." Selene chose one, an old shirt, tie-dyed blue. She pressed it to Lake's face.

"Breathe," she said. "It's like sun and wind and green things. Don't you see?"

"Vernelle would never be caught *dead* in this," Lake said as she took off yesterday's shirt and let it drop into the basket. She turned away from Selene. Even though the family, all of them, swam and bathed together in the river, Lake was aware of how big she was—broader-shouldered, taller, heavier thighed, bigger everywhere, she thought—compared to Selene. She'd inherited Ty's sturdiness and large bones, his light brown hair, even his nose, which he said was Roman and which he liked. As she hurried into the shirt, she breathed in all those fragrances Selene mentioned. Lake felt a twinge of guilt.

Selene lifted Lake's hair out of the inside of the shirt and when she hugged her, Lake hugged back, hard and sure, the way she'd always done—even when she didn't know why.

"So what else is new?" Selene said and gave the guitar a quick strum.

"We got someone new last night after dinner," Lake said, remembering the way Sun Dog seemed to fill up the whole room. Remembering his cartwheels and his moon shadow, his funny way of singing. Remembering the way he called her a "green-eyed lady."

"Who? A family? A gardener, I hope?"

"No. A guy. Alone. I couldn't tell how old. Twenty, twenty-one, maybe. Maybe even Ty's age," Lake said.

"Wonderful." Selene gave the guitar a quick, angry strum. "Just what we need."

"He knows all about Barataria and he's been at Cosmic Freedom Farm. He knows all these people who know Ty and . . ."

"What can he do?" Selene said. "Did Ty—did anyone— ask him what he can *do*?"

Lake shrugged. "He has a guitar. Twelve-string."

"What? No pyramids or crystals? Good grief, Lake! Everyone has a guitar. We all play guitars. We've done that forever!" Selene said.

"He's . . . this one's . . . different, I think." Lake pictured his shattered mirror eyes and his trim black beard and tried not to admit her feelings even to herself.

"At least it's not one of those sick girls with a baby on her back who thinks this is heaven."

"Maybe he'll pull his share," Lake said.

"Maybe." Selene bent her head over her guitar, twisting the keys, tuning it. "Let's not count on it."

"Mom." It was funny. Lake realized she called Selene "Mom" only when she was angry—when she was the most honest, Ty would have said.

"Mom, isn't that what we're supposed to believe around

15

here? Rules to live by? Share what we've got? Give everyone a chance? Take time to teach?"

"Okay. Okay. I guess I'll have to trust Tyler on this one . . ."

Selene flipped her salt-and-pepper gray hair back off one shoulder, strummed the guitar, and sang a few notes. Lake didn't understand how that rich, vibrant voice could come out of such a small head and doll-like face. She watched Selene's small, doll mouth move over her large teeth and she knew why people couldn't seem to take their eyes off her. Maybe they were trying to figure out why her eyes were so round, what made her mouth move that way, and whether she was really beautiful or just odd.

"You haven't done much singing lately. Sounds nice," Lake said.

"I've been thinking a lot lately." Selene put down her guitar. "I don't know why, but thinking a lot about when you were born."

"When I was born?" Lake wasn't sure she wanted to hear this. "Wasn't it just like the way everyone else is born? Conceived?"

"No, no," Selene said. "Listen. I need to . . . It was at our very first commune, the one we drove out to after the assassination of President Kennedy? Well, we thought this place was exactly what we were looking for, but the first thing, the day we got there, we were told right off that all couples, married or not, had to live apart. You know, until the group decided we were spiritual, enlightened enough to have a true marriage. So, we slept in separate dorms almost six months," Selene told Lake, smiling. "We were so young. It was unforgivable."

"Why didn't you just sneak out? Just leave?" Lake said.

"We never even thought about it. We just had this . . . commitment to all those . . . ideals." Selene shook her head, as if she couldn't believe it either.

"Finally, after all their interminable talk, they gave us permission. It was so humiliating . . . but we didn't think so then. Funny."

Selene picked up the stack of clean towels and put them on the shelf. Lake didn't understand why her mother had to tell this story now—and to her—after all this time. But she listened and tried to imagine her parents' new marriage ceremony performed out on a mountaintop somewhere, so different from the formal wedding beneath the stained glass windows in the Episcopal church where Selene had gone to Sunday school all of her life. Selene told Lake the story as if it had happened to someone else, not herself.

"We did what was required there," she said, "but as soon as we could after the group wedding, we left in the dead of night. And we took you, Lakey, already blooming inside me."

Selene laid her head on Lake's shoulder.

"You know, we wanted to sort out all those old attitudes we had, confront all that stuff in our heads, but what Ty couldn't stand was someone telling him what he could think. It was right after that we found the Cosmic Freedom Farm. . . . Out of the frying pan and into the fire, only we didn't know it then," Selene said.

Lake jumped off the table and started outside. She didn't know what she was supposed to say to Selene and didn't want to hear any more confidences. After all, Selene was her mother, not some girl from school who makes friends by giving away too many secrets, too soon. All she could think about was her urgent beginnings, while the whole world watched. Maybe that's why she had turned out to be so secretive, so private, so territorial.

Selene followed her outside. "Okay, I hope you'll understand. I just want you to be aware of things," she said. "Hey, come on, help me with these sheets."

She handed one end of a sheet to Lake. Years ago they had made up what they called a folding dance. They faced each other like partners in an old-fashioned minuet, then came together, holding the white sheet, and then danced apart as the sheet billowed out between them. Now Selene hummed their special song as she took the folded sheet from Lake. There was a strong rush of kinship for her mother, and Lake felt suddenly that it was right, after all, to farm the land, to share and work on the mutual understanding and self-awareness that everyone talked about.

Back inside the washhouse, Selene picked up the guitar again; she seemed to forget that Lake was there as she bent over the dark wooden instrument. In her deep, rich voice she sang, *"Sometimes I feel like a motherless child/sometimes I feel . . ."*

The door pushed open. Wearing the same old cutoff jeans and the big buckle at his waist, Sun Dog walked into the washhouse carrying his big twelve-string. His wet hair curled away from his face like a ruffled hat.

"Hey, green-eyed lady," he said. "Who's this sweet singing woman here?"

Without waiting for an answer, Sun Dog turned to Selene. "You don't look like no motherless child to me," he said. "You look like you belong to the earth and you sound like an angel."

Selene put her guitar down and picked up another towel.

"I'm takin' my time," he said, "looking around here today. I'm new around here, new as the day," he said.

"This is where we keep the clothes . . ." Selene said.

"Yeah." He shook his head. "Wow! Man!"

He walked around the room with his hands clasped behind his back, bending at the waist, looking at things as if they were pictures on a museum wall and he was studying art.

Lake went outside to bring in dry T-shirts, hanging limp and still on the line strung between trees. She folded them slowly and dropped them in the wash basket, listening hard until she heard the sound of her mother's guitar come through the open door. And then came the deep, throaty sound of Sun Dog's twelve-string seeping into those first tentative chords. Carrying the wicker basket heaped with clean clothes, Lake stood in the open doorway, listening. They were sitting on the table.

"Sing me a little something," he said.

Selene hesitated only a moment and then began to sing, *"Amazing grace, how sweet the sound . . ."*

When Sun Dog joined in, the music sounded as if he and Selene had been singing together all their lives; he knew when to change keys, when to vary the tempo, when to repeat a line. Selene didn't stop or look up, but her voice changed ever so slightly to blend with the rich throb of Sun Dog's guitar. Lake felt the hair raise up on her neck and goose bumps rise on her arms. Just then, Selene plucked a wrong chord and frowned.

Then, looking serious and afffected, she began to sing in

her Joan Baez voice. Without hesitation, without missing a single note, Sun Dog switched, too, and sang in his high, funny voice. They sounded like Baez and Bob Dylan from the sixties, who Ty and Selene listened to sometimes. Laughing at themselves, they switched to the songs that people sang around camp fires or at camp when they were children. "Down by the Riverside" and "Old McDonald." Lake sang along with them until their laughter took over from the music.

3

A few days later Lake came out of the Children's House and there was Sun Dog, with his thumbs hooked into his belt loops, gazing up at the unpainted building. He was all over the place these days. It wasn't just the way he told Selene she ought to get a singing job somewhere and not bury herself here at Barataria. No, he moved in on everyone. First he found a way to repair the tractor when no one else, not even Ty, could do it. Then he fixed the stopped-up sink for Lana. After that Ty told him he could drive the pickup any time he wanted to. He's taking over, Lake thought. Now he was there on the front stoop of the Children's House unloading something onto the porch.

"Hey, what's happening?" Lake said. She put her hands on her hips. "This is kids' territory, you know?"

"What's happening is paint," he said.

He leaned into the pickup, which he had backed close to the front stoop. Picking up metal cans, he carried them two at a time to the porch. The thin wire handles clinked against the cans when he dropped them. Lake saw the way his hair fringed, curled up around his face when he took off his black hat and hung it on a tree limb, saw the way he smiled more to himself than to her. He looked as happy as Tyler had the first time he'd done his own hay-making from start to finish, from planting to mowing to raking and storing, a kind of secret happiness.

"Paint? You're talking about paint?" she said. "What for? What needs painting around here?"

She looked at the house with its old wood, weathered and gray, the funny way the porch was built from trees. Someone had used tree stumps with the bark peeled off to hold up the porch roof and the railing, and stubs of branches still showed here and there. It was irregular and unusual, but Lake liked it. It made the Children's House, her house, different from the others in town.

"Why, I had it in mind to paint your house here for you. Today," he said. "Well, not the whole house, mind you. Just the porch. The front porch. I have taken a liking to your front porch."

He took a screwdriver out of the toolbox in the truck bed and pried the lid off a can of paint. It was bright blue, as blue as the low-growing scylla that bloomed all around the yard, bloomed so early some years that snow was still on the ground.

"Well, who said you could?" Lake said. "You've got to talk it over with somebody, don't you? Meeting is tomorrow. Wouldn't it be. . . ? I mean—talk it over?"

"I am talking it over. With you."

"Well, put the lid back then," she said.

"That blue is supposed to lure you, girl," he said, and went back to the truck.

"You think just because you fixed the tractor? Found that old freezer in the dump and got it going? Just because you . . ." Her voice faded. Her heart pounded until she remembered the flowers. Not wild flowers from the mead-

22

ows and pastures, but real florist's flowers he'd arranged for the dinner table in fruit jars. He claimed the florist in town gave them to him.

"Fine," she said. "But, what right have you. . . ?" She stepped between him and the porch.

He gave her a long look. "I got no rights in this world. None but what somebody else says I got. Nobody does. That's the way they got the world set up, honey." He smiled, and the gap in his white teeth showed again.

She tried not to look at him because when she did something weird happened inside her body. If I catch his eye, she thought, he will know. Besides, even if she wanted to be as kind and unjudging as Tyler and Andy would be, it was the kids' house, wasn't it? Not his?

He didn't answer, just picked up a brush out of the truck and went around her toward the can of blue paint, waiting there like a patch of sky.

"Well, hell, Lakey honey," he said. "Don't you think we ought to have a little fun? Fix this place up?"

He threw out his arm taking in the old, unpainted house, the crazy front porch.

"You can't just . . . decide," she said. "By yourself."

This time she looked straight into his eyes, which gleamed, shone in the sunlight.

"I won't decide," he said. "*We* decide. You vote. Right now. Say yes, green-eyed lady, and we'll have us a time!"

He knelt down on one knee, found the screwdriver in his jacket, and pried the lid off another can. It was pink this time. She realized that the cans were only half full. Every one had been used to paint someone's kitchen or bathroom, or to paint toys in bright colors. Drips of red, green, peach, yellow, or lavender streaked each can.

"Where'd you get all this junk?" she asked.

23

"A painter. Guy in town. He tossed them out."

She followed him onto the porch steps.

"It'll be every color in the rainbow," she said.

"All right!" he said, and tried to shake her hand, but she put it behind her back. "Now you get the idea!"

His eyes with that moist layer shining on them were so full of so many things that she thought maybe he was right. Had she become too serious, more conscious of the rules on the farm than the spirit of it? Did she really want to take the fun out of everything?

"Brushes," she said. "You haven't got enough brushes anyhow."

"So say you," he said. "Look here." He opened the truck door, and wrapped in an old flannel shirt from the communal closet were enough brand-new paintbrushes of all sizes to give everyone a brush. He threw her one.

It still had a price sticker on the handle: $2.48. He dipped his brush into the blue, lifted it up, and let the paint run down his wrist and into the palm of his hand.

He touched his brush to one of the gnarled uprights. She watched him, undecided about whether to call Tyler, until Sun Dog had paint on his boots and in his hair, and he had rubbed the streak of blue paint down his leg as a child might do.

The colors on the cans began to sort themselves out in her mind: sea green, the lavender of iris, the red of a cardinal. She tried to imagine the porch as Sun Dog did.

She took a deep breath and let it out slowly. She dipped her brush into a can of green paint.

While they worked the sun worked in its own way, came around the sky and added its own gold to the house as it shone into the windows. Kesey came out of the barn, stopping at the big tree where Sun Dog had hung his hat an hour ago.

"Hey, now that is cool," he said. "Fab-you-lous!"

"Yeah, we thought so," Sun Dog said.

"Can I do some?" Kesey said, picking up a discarded brush.

"Why not?" Sun Dog said.

"Tom Sawyer," Lake said.

She put her brush down and walked to the edge of the yard, back where the grass was greening up. From there it looked like a marvelous modern painting, like a poster in an art store window. At the other end of the porch, Kesey, holding two brushes in his teeth, painted neat stripes of yellow, pink, and green on the rail. Soon Andy and Lana, Free and Selene joined in. There wasn't much said, only "May I borrow the blue?" or "Do you like yellow here?"

They didn't stop for dinner and they didn't stop at painting the porch either. The older children like Chad came to help, and Sun Dog put them to work painting the side of the house. Before anyone realized it Andy had brought a stepladder out from the barn and painted the upstairs window frames and their mullions purple and orange. Ty and Selene painted red shutters downstairs where no shutters were. It was Lake who painted a rainbow across the front door and Sun Dog who painted a bright white sun above it.

When Lana told the children not to drip so much paint on their clothes, they took them off and hung them on tree branches, and soon the whole family did the same thing. Someone brought a bottle of the grape wine they had made last year, and when they drank it out of the bottle the wine ran down their chins as purple as paint. They turned on the truck headlights and the big yard light to see by and sang until they were hoarse and breathless.

Lake saw two pickup trucks pass by and slow down up on the ridge road in front of the house. Not until they got to the top of the ridge did they stop and turn off their headlights. Lake would only think of it later when it meant something.

4

Lana and Free squeezed over to make room for Lake in the big circle on the living room floor. The family was all there, sitting shoulder to shoulder, some with their legs crossed as if in meditation. Meditation was something some of them practiced: facing the sun at dawn, into the sunset at twilight. But tonight they weren't meditating. This was meeting, and meeting was never quiet or spiritual and often lasted way into the night. One good thing about it, Lake decided, was that everyone was in a good mood after the painting party. Even Lana had gotten into the swing of the house painting. She called Sun Dog the Pied Piper of Barataria. She was right. The children followed him around all week, and Lake wished she could ask him to hold her, sing to her the way they did as they trailed after him with a toy to fix.

Lake was late; she had been in the barn helping Ty knock down the partitions between stalls, building extra sleeping space. She hadn't hurried. Meeting never started on time anyway. Nobody minded if you were late or if you showed at all. Carrying mugs of coffee, the family members milled around as if the living room were a bus station and they were each taking a different bus.

Seated cross-legged between Lana and Free, who talked about whether it was dry enough to plow the oats field, Lake leaned against the sofa as far from the wood stove as she could get. Someone had built up the fire against the early spring freeze and now the room felt too warm. That's the way it was. You didn't always get things your way in a community like Barataria. The smell of wood smoke on Free's flannel shirt, of steam boiling out of the rusty iron pot on the back burner, and of the steamy room reminded Lake that it soon would be time to cut the alfalfa field and plant corn, and real spring would finally be here.

The sofa Lake leaned against was as swaybacked as an old horse, but it was filled with soft pillows embroidered or needlepointed by Barataria people. There were posters taped to every wall admonishing everyone to "Grow where you are planted" or "Make love not war." Book shelves lined the walls all the way to the high ceiling and were built over every door frame. Below the front windows orange-crate shelves held back-issues of *The Farm Journal*, where Ty and Selene first read the ad about this place. It was a wonderful room, Lake thought. She loved the golden, muted light shining from kerosene lamps lighted to save electricity, loved the jumble of pillows piled on the floor and the way twilight waited outside the uncurtained windows.

Some of the children played in the hammocks hung across the corner of the room, a reminder of the hammock business they had had years ago. Lake remembered the blisters on Selene's fingers from hours of pulling, tying, knotting, tightening heavy cotton string in the community workshop set up in the barn. Halsey's baby fell out when the hammock was rocked too high. Tyler ran to pick her up, and holding her close to his heart, patted and crooned until her crying stopped. Then he lifted the others out of the swinging hammocks.

"I need you to go outside to play. And take the dogs, too, please," he said.

Chased toward the door by all the children, the dogs slid and bumbled around the room, rumpling up throw rugs, barking wildly, and thumping their thick tails against the floor. Chad and Kesey picked up Andy's dog, Prudence, and laid him in the empty hammock. Andy's dog was only one of the large furry mixed-breed dogs that lived at the farm. Most answered to no one, had no special name, roamed in groups, scrounged food from barn and house and field. Over protests that Prudence wasn't female and should have a proper name like "Rover" or "Shep," Andy called him "Prudence."

"For the way we live," Andy said.

Prudence struggled and barked and seemed to swim in the air, with his legs sticking out of the netting. In the confusion, Andy knocked a stack of magazines and books off a shelf. Prudence barked louder, and the children came back into the meeting room and ran around while the adults, laughing and yelling at the children, hurried to pick up books and help the dog.

This was the part Lake liked best: the laughing and teasing, the dogs and the golden room, the good food smells. She recognized their mutual understanding, got high on the warmth of all their love for each other. This was the life they all had imagined when they came here, the reason they had left schools and jobs way back in the sixties, why they had hung on to the dream so long. When it was like this, she didn't think so much about, and feel so full of desire for, something else. That kind of thinking seemed wasteful somehow. She wrapped her arms around herself and smiled with pleasure.

"Hey, let's get started," she said.

Because Andy was the one who called the meeting, he spoke first.

"Listen," he said. "According to our plan, the sleeping rooms in the small barn are supposed to be ready to sleep in by now."

"Well, you can kiss that good-bye." Lana folded her arms across her chest.

"Yeah," Andy said. "Plus, if it ever warms up, it's almost time to make hay. We're running out of time."

"And space," Lana said.

Andy swung his large body around to face the group squarely, just the way he did everything.

"In the meantime, people, I've got to have some room"—he took a deep breath and sat down hard on the couch—"to breathe." It was a long speech for Andy Johnson.

Andy was a big man, dressed in a blue work shirt and jeans like everyone else in the room. Everyone looks alike, Lake thought, except for a few scarves or belts or hand-knitted sweaters. Even all the women looked alike with long straight hair parted in the middle and jeans and T-shirts. The only variety was in the sayings on the shirts.

Tyler said, "I know it's tough." He spread his hands out, palms up. He shrugged. "We're tight. Real tight. Tight until, I don't know for sure—at least three, four months." He looked at Andy for corroboration, but Andy didn't respond. "It's the old story. Time and money. Maybe we have the time, but we ain't got the do-re-mi." He sang a little off-key, the way he always did.

30

"It's lumber we need," Free said.

"Man, it's cash we need," Andy said.

Tyler smiled his wide smile and his teeth showed between his lips. His eyes seemed to melt and grow and take Andy in. Andy was just like everyone else on the farm, they all listened when Ty spoke. But now Andy grumbled, muttered into his fiery beard.

"Speak up. You got something else to say?" Tyler's smile was gone now. "That's what we do here, remember. No holds barred."

"I said what I wanted to say." Andy had a hammer stuck in the loop on his jeans, and it bounced as he paced the floor.

"That's not all we want to say," Lana said. "I mean . . . that's what this meeting is all about. Space."

She put her hand on Lake's shoulder to stand up. She turned in a circle looking for Ty.

"You and Selene got more space than you need. More than anyone. If those rooms in the barn aren't going to be finished, then you've got to share, Ty. That's about it."

That's not totally it, Lake thought. Andy and Lana want to move in together now, and this is the only way to do it.

"Anyone else? Anyone else think we've got too much space?" Tyler said.

"Well," Free Adams began. He had a fringe of long, gray-brown hair around his ears, and with his high bony forehead and thick glasses he looked like the college professor he had once been. "Yeah, Ty. I agree. I think it's time to reallocate space. We've got our very top limit of people here now. It's understood that Sun Dog is in? Probation is over. He's in, right?"

Everyone applauded and cheered. Sun Dog struggled to

31

his feet, ducked his head, and bowed with his hat in his hand like one of the Three Musketeers.

"It isn't like when we bought the land and started the farm," Andy said, turning to Ty.

But Andy was wrong about buying the land. Tyler had been the only one with money back then, money enough to buy land. His parents had died when he was in college, and he inherited all their money. No one ever said how much it was, but it came to him as regular as the seasons. It was as if it had been planted somewhere and twice a year it produced its bountiful crop. He had made up his mind back in the sixties that money was only a commodity, so he used it as others used their labors, for the betterment of the Barataria Farm.

People called him a truster, and Lake thought that was a perfect name for him.

Tyler never spoke about the money, but the family didn't forget. They showed that they remembered by giving Ty and Selene two whole rooms upstairs in the Big House for their own use. They used the extra room for Selene's looms and yarns and Ty's maps and desk, his file cabinet, and farming books.

When the vote was taken, it was unanimous. Selene and Ty would have to move out of one of their rooms upstairs, and Lana and Andy could move right in. To smooth the transition, everyone agreed that they'd make room in the barn for Ty's desk and for Selene's weaving supplies and help them move. When it was over people hugged each other and smiled and said it was fair. They owned everything and nothing, they said—the houses, the barns, the well pump, the old car, the ornery tractor, even the river, curling white and noisy down the hill.

No one seemed to notice Selene's look, her eyes shining

with tears. Ty tried to make her look at him from across the room, but she stared into the open door of the wood stove instead.

"Hey, quiet!" Lana clapped her hands for order. "We've got something else on the agenda before we break up. I've got one thing to say and that is *hot water*."

"Not again," Ty said. "We're tight on cash, Lana, you know that better than anyone." It was Lana who worked at a desk in a kitchen nook behind the pantry, assigning jobs, keeping records, counting up work hours.

Lake sighed. She'd heard all this so many times. It was the same whether they talked about water power or buying another cow or weaving hammocks or raising mushrooms to sell. About the only thing they had ever agreed on without a lot of talk was Christmas tree seedlings two years ago, and the trees had died in the drought.

Free spoke up. "Face it, folks. If we want lumber and nails and stuff, then we pay. We're going to have to get real jobs, people. Now."

"No way. We're supposed to be self-sufficient," someone said.

So there it was again. No one accepted anything, questioned everything. Lake listened as long as she could. She lay down in one of the hammocks. As the hammock rose and fell voices blurred, blended into one, and Lake drifted into sleep. She dreamed of the little pile of hand-ground flour growing like a pyramid under Selene's hand. She heard her mother's low voice, thick with sleep, say, "I'm not really in North Dakota, it is not 1879, and I am not my own grandmother."

Like an orchestra tuning itself, the *plink*, *plink* sound of a banjo and a guitar and tambourines intruded on Lake's

33

dream. Meeting was over and now the dancing party could begin. It was pure dark outside now, and the tall uncurtained windows reflected the golden light from the kerosene lamps that had been lit. Lake lay there for a moment, taking in the smells of gum-soled boots standing close to the stove, the crackle of apple logs burning, sweat and garlic and babies' wet diapers. Through her half-opened eyes, she saw the bulky shadows of the big men and the long-haired women and the children cast upon the walls. Somehow, she dreamed, with our long hair and heavy clothes, we all look like cavemen and women in the golden firelight. She dozed there in the hammock until Kesey and Chad dumped her out onto the floor.

"Come on, girl. It's party time!" Kesey said, helping her up.

Andy pushed back the sofa and chairs, and the music and dancing began. When the children heard the sounds, they came back indoors, threading their way in and out of the dancers while the dogs barked and chased them. There was a bongo drum beating, beating. Someone—Lake couldn't see who—opened the front door, and with Sun Dog leading the way everyone danced out into the hall and right out the front door. When Ty handed her a torch from the fireplace, Lake ran ahead to light the way. In the sudden cold, so biting after the warm house, she felt light-headed and giddy, overcome with noise and music, the rhythm of her heart marking time with the drum's pounding. Kesey tossed his torch into the brush pile and soon fire boomed up into the air. Everything was warm now. Lake danced with everyone, turning, swaying, holding them. She danced alone, watching sparks burn white and then fall to the ground like spent fireworks. She was akin to the universe, she imagined, spinning, spinning, spinning. A universe made for this one joyous spectacle of a night.

When she stopped her dizzy twirl, Sun Dog had turned some cartwheels the way he did that first night, and the children fell down in delirious laughter. The bonfire flickered into the children's eyes as they took in the sight of all the adults dancing wild and strong in the firelight. Out of doors, with trees towering overhead and the river streaming by and the fire leaping, Lake imagined again the cave dwellers coming out of the shadows and into the light, appearing and disappearing like ghosts. She felt as if a new part of her body had opened to let in light and mystery, fire and knowingness. Maybe a whole new world was about to begin, she thought, the one they all envisioned.

Sun Dog swung Chad around and around by his hands so that the boy's body sometimes barely skimmed the ground, sometimes flew high in the air, while he screamed and swore with fear and delight. Sun Dog had taken off his heavy shirt and his skin shone bronze in the yellow light. Then Sun Dog and Andy lumbered around the fire like two bears, grinning and dancing. Tyler's blond hair seemed on fire around his long face as he watched it all. Lake stopped long enough to look for Selene, but she was nowhere to be found.

Sun Dog stopped the resounding dance with Andy and moved toward Lake. He carried a piece of charred wood, pencil thin.

"Come here, little green-eyed girl. Let me look. Are you green-eyed at night, too?" he said.

"Sure, I guess. I don't . . ." she said, and shrugged. "Isn't this great?" She waved both her arms, taking in the fire and the friends and the world, she thought. She smiled at him and felt her face grow red, not just with fire.

"Yeah. Come here," he said as he took her face in his hand.

His fingers were rough and smelled of wood smoke. With the piece of charred wood, he drew pictures on her forehead, her cheeks, brushing back her hair, holding her chin. Tyler came then, too, took the piece of wood and drew suns and moons on Sun Dog's shoulders.

"Like Lake's," he said.

The children circled them, begging for their own moon, until soon everyone was touched by the strange night, everyone.

5

Lake headed toward the two rooms at the top of the stairs that had always, since the very beginning of Barataria, belonged to her parents. Now, as a result of last night's meeting, Lana and Andy had permission to put their things up here in one of those rooms. They drew straws for first pick and, of course, when she got the longest straw, Lana took the big "loom room," which left the smaller room under the eaves for Ty and Selene.

Lake hadn't liked the meeting or the vote or the choosing of straws, and she had held her own hands clasped together in her lap. No one seemed to notice that she didn't vote. Perhaps even Selene had not noticed. Maybe Selene was too busy thinking about her old room up in Michigan in her mother's house, the spacious place with two closets that Lake remembered so clearly. Still, Lake told herself, the new room arrangement was voted on fair and square, wasn't it? That's the way we do things at Barataria, isn't it? All for one and one for all?

Now Lake peered into her parents' bedroom, the room they'd keep. It was dark, nestlike, with a clear view of the river through low windows from the massive antique oak bed. The marriage bed, Ty called it. Its carved headboard had been pushed against the back wall out of its usual place. The wall-hanging above it was off center now, off center like Selene, who had been working on the piece off and on for years, adding colored beads or feathers or weaving in yarn she dyed herself from goldenrod or beets, anything she could find in the woods and fields. Somehow Lake had never been able to look at it too closely. It was as if she might read her mother's diary there. The hanging seemed made of her parents' secrets about their lovemaking, their fights and reconciliations.

Selene had said once that it was her journal and therefore would never be finished, not until she and Ty were finished. And that would be never, she said.

With the bed out of place everything in the room looked different. Nothing ever stayed the same, Lake thought, and leaned against the open door. Why this was so she didn't understand, and she felt that this was an important part of life that she would have to think about. She just didn't have time to think about it now. Everyone would arrive any minute now to help carry things that wouldn't fit into this room out to the barn and bring Lana's and Andy's stuff up the narrow steps.

"Hey?" she said. "Where are you guys?"

When no one answered her call, she went across the hall into the square room Ty called the "office-cum-loom room." Lake expected to find Selene there, bent over the floor loom, winding warp threads onto the beam; or maybe on the window seat, looking out across the road and into the hills, fingering weird minor chords on her guitar. Or maybe, Lake wished, Ty might be at his desk, plotting out which field should go into pasture and which one was ready to take planting. But instead Tyler stood in the middle of the room with an empty desk drawer in each hand.

"Hey! You! Everyone will be here to help in a minute. You ready for them? They're gonna expect you to be ready," Lake said. She tried to sound matter-of-fact, even cheerful.

"No, hell, no, I'm not ready. I don't know . . . I can't . . ." Ty said. "Maybe I'll put my desk in the kitchen near Lana's. What do you think?"

He turned around in a circle, almost in a dance—a dance of grief, Lake thought.

Even though the air upstairs was heavy and humid, Lake felt chilled. Everything she touched felt damp, almost cold. She searched through a couple of boxes for a screwdriver and, for the first time, she saw her mother seated cross-legged on the floor behind the loom. Sagging wicker baskets filled with hanks of yarn surrounded her, and someone had tossed books in on top of it all as if to say, who cares, anyway? Selene emptied the contents of an old straw bag into her full-skirted lap: a little vial of liquid silver, smooth river stones from a Havasupai Indian reservation, a picture postcard of Sitting Bull in full regalia, a John Kennedy campaign button, a mouth harp, and a yellowed color photograph of laughing young men and women with long hair and beads and feathers. Ty and Selene were in the picture. Selene stood up and dumped her skirtful of old memories into an empty wastebasket. She left the photo on the floor where it landed.

"We're ready," Selene said, and picked up a wrench and a screwdriver, flourishing them like swords.

Lake hated to see the looms torn down. She liked to come up here in the high-ceilinged room and watch her mother throw the heddles, hear the steady *thump, thump, thump* of the foot pedal, and see the colors grow as if they came from Selene's fingertips onto the warp.

"We'll get them set up in the barn for you, okay?" Lake said, bending to look into her mother's face. Her hair wasn't tied back and it shaded her eyes, a curtained hiding place. Lake couldn't be sure about how her mother felt to be leaving this room for Andy and Lana. At meeting she'd said, maybe only a little too loudly, "Sure, don't worry about it. All's fair in love . . ." But later Lake heard her say, "Okay, Ty, okay. Don't get yourself in a snit. Whatever happens happens."

When Ty untaped his maps from the wall, pale squares showed up behind them on the darker wall. He snapped a rubber band around the rolled-up tube of maps he had drawn so carefully. They pictured the topography of the fields, what was planted in them, the pH of the soil, and records about the yield of each acre. He laid them on his old swivel chair and rolled it toward the door.

There was a sudden rush of voices and the sound of boots clumping up the bare wooden stairs.

"I guess this must be the place and this must be the day," Lana said. Lake could almost smell Lana's feeling of ownership. She was trying hard not to let it show, and that only made it worse.

Now Sun Dog picked up pieces of Selene's loom, passed them to Free, and on to the next person in line. Eventually the beams and rods moved down the stairs, out through the kitchen, and onto the side porch. Lake stared out the window and watched Halsey toss the loom into the old pickup, parked with the bed level to the porch. Lake wanted to cry for her mother and for herself, too.

Sun Dog picked up a cardboard box and said, "Hey, Lake, you're doggin' it. Get busy, girl."

When he touched her bare arm, she dropped her basket of yarn. All the balls rolled silently, softly across the hall and back into the bedroom. She stooped to pick them up.

"You're interrupting the flow," Sun Dog said, almost whispering. He was making fun of her, but the look in his eyes told her he thought she was fine, maybe even beautiful, she thought. Why, without saying a word, did he make her feel so good? She knew he made everyone feel that way, but she wanted to believe it was just her. When she found the last ball of yarn, she stood up. Sun Dog was gone and Lana and Selene were standing together in the center of the room.

"—you guys just bring your bedroom stuff in here. Bring it in here," Lana was saying. "This is your real room. Keep it. Even with your bed and dresser in here, there's plenty of room for Ty's desk. Maybe not the looms, but . . ."

Andy came upstairs then and Lana grabbed his hand.

"Listen," she said. "Here's a great idea."

When she finished telling him, he smiled so hard Lake thought he would burst. His whole face shone with sweat and happiness. He hollered down to everyone, Sun Dog and all the others, "Hold it, we got a change in the plans here."

Selene stopped taking her posters off the wall. The Matisse forms in green, red, and blue seemed to dance around the room.

Lake knew that Ty and Selene wanted to stay in this room with the window seat looking out over the back fields and the river, and she knew, too, that Andy and Lana wanted them to do it so they wouldn't have to feel guilty and selfish for the one-sided vote at meeting. Of course the bed would have to be squeezed against the wall and Selene's looms would have to go, but it could be done.

"It would make everyone feel better, Ty," Lake said.

Lake wanted Tyler to say yes, wanted to see his desk in front of the big windows where it belonged, where he could see the farm spread out before him.

Selene didn't say yes, but she put Ty's lamp back on the corner of the desk where it belonged. Ty bent down to unroll the rug, a wedding present from his parents. Selene smiled.

"Never let it be said we wouldn't help out a friend in need," Tyler said.

Without knowing exactly how it happened or who started it, Lake found herself caught up in a big hug with all four of them. They opened their circle to take her in and she felt their strong fragrance and their bodies and their comradeship. They laughed and cried and cursed each other, and Selene looked . . . Lake couldn't read her mother's look. But she thought everything would be fine now. She realized again how hard they all worked at being open and honest and fair with each other, with the world actually. She wanted to be like them, open and relaxed. How had she forgotten what they were trying to do and how important it was? Lake took a deep breath and let it out through her mouth.

"Reelaaaxx," she said.

The two couples went into the room across the hall and did another bucket brigade, moving clothes, more books, towels, pillows, dresser drawers, and then the heavy bedstead itself was taken down, the mattress jockeyed across the hall and onto the frame. While they were across the hall in the small room, Lake unrolled the rest of Ty's rug with her foot, revealing more and more of the otherworldly trees and flowers, the brilliant colors. She went into the empty room to help move the last bag of clothes.

Lana had climbed onto a chair and was taking Selene's wall-hanging from its wire hanger. Bits of colored glass and broken mirror glinted and flashed like little lightnings.

"Don't take that down," Selene said, pulling at Lana's skirt. "I want you and Andy to have it."

Lana stared up at the hanging. "Well, if you're sure, I'd love to have it. Maybe it will bring Andy and me . . . luck," Lana said.

Lana and Selene hugged again, and Lana said, "Hey, you're my sister and I love you. This is going to be okay, really it is."

"I know," Selene said. "I don't know what gets into me sometimes. I mean—what could be better?"

Lake couldn't imagine why her mother had given the wall hanging to Lana. Of course it was because Lana had been so generous. Still, in spite of her mother's gratitude, how could she give her own work, the work that was so intimate? Lake turned to leave. The photograph that had fallen to the floor earlier was still on the floor. She bent to pick it up, staring at her mother's face. Selene looked younger, of course, but it was something else, some openness that was missing now, even when Selene was trying to act like her old self. Why did everything Selene say lately seem to be playacting?

6

Lake's job this morning was to measure one-by-sixes, mark them with Ty's blue pencil, and then cut boards into the right length for Andy. She laid a board across the sawhorses, measured it, and let the saw bite into the pine. She loved the smell of new lumber, the curve of the saw handle in her hand, the soft, flat feel of sawdust piling up at her feet like sand at a beach. Earlier there were two-by-fours and one-by-sixes stacked crisscross atop each other waiting in the yard. Now there was only this one last board and naked-looking white and yellow grass where the rest of the boards had lain so long. What would happen now? They had bought all the lumber they could afford and they had tried to eke it out, make it last, make no mistakes, measure right. But now they'd come to the end and Ty would have to figure out what to do next. The extra sleeping rooms they were building in the barn weren't even half done. Lake slicked back her hair, rubbed her sticky hands across her face, and smelled the pine resin on her fingers. She'd have to tell Tyler.

On her way into the barn to find him, she imagined what Selene would say when she found out. Selene had tried to be a good sport, but she wasn't really. She didn't joke around with Sun Dog or sing with him as often and as freely, and even though she'd moved her looms out of the barn, she hadn't set them up in the Children's House yet. She kept saying "I will, don't rush me."

Lake muttered to herself. Just when the work was going so well. Just when Ty seemed so focused, as though this was the real dream. . . . Everyone working toward one common goal. Was it always going to be like this? Never having anything finished? Never having enough money? How could she plan ahead for college or anything?

Inside the barn she smelled the odor of dust and manure, of musty oats and rotting hay. It was colder inside the barn than outside, and she put her hands under her armpits to warm them. Across from her there was a yellow square of light where morning sun shone through the opened door onto dust motes suspended in the air. The barn seemed to breathe out emptiness, time. Everything seemed muted, dim, patient somehow. She heard the soft *thud, thud* of Ty's hammer against old wood, the flutter of swallows as they flew up suddenly and then resettled themselves on the beams. Lake loved the barn, the cobwebby ceilings high above her where spiders hung like trapeze artists by their mouths. She loved the wide, worn boards in the uneven floor, the stone sills, the animal smells.

She touched one of the hand-hewn oak posts where adz marks still showed. She wondered what Mr. Van Emmerline might think if he could travel forward ninety years to see what was happening to his family farm. If Mr. Van Emmerline, whose picture still hung in the dining room of the farmhouse, were reincarnated, he would

45

come back as Ty, Lake thought, Ty who was so at home here.

She handed the board to her father, looked closely at him. He didn't look like the bearded Mr. Van Emmerline. He looked like Tyler, sturdy, high-cheekboned with his blue, blue eyes.

"That's it," she said. "That's the last piece."

Before Ty answered Selene appeared, squinting into the dimness, followed by some of the children. They carried skillets of corn bread, thick slices of the last of their onions, bowls and spoons on trays. Selene carried a pot of white soup beans with a towel wrapped around the handle.

"Come and get it while it's hot," she said.

She stood there with the square of yellow light behind her, and Lake couldn't see her face, only her silhouetted form as she ladled soup into thick white bowls and broke off hunks of warm, crusty bread for everyone. Dragging a sledgehammer by the handle, Ty came out of the dusty gloom. When it was his turn he took the bowl of soup from her and sat down on a bale of straw-colored hay, rubbing the dust off his hands along his thighs. They didn't speak. Without stopping to eat, the way she usually did, Selene went back to the Big House. The screen door slammed hard behind her.

Slowly Ty wiped his mouth with the back of his hand and followed her into the house. Everyone stopped eating, didn't look up or talk, just sat there, listening to every word her parents said to each other. Lake wanted to hide, fly up to the hay loft with the swallows and the spiders. But she could only listen along with the others. Somehow this was worse, listening in like this, than the open quarreling in meeting or on a job with everyone taking part.

"—the wood is gone, isn't it?" Selene was saying. "I heard Lake."

Ty's answer was too low for them to overhear. But then Selene's voice came louder, insistent.

"Why can't you see? It's so obvious," she said. "We're just spinning our wheels here. No. No, we're going backward. But you can't see!"

"You're right. I know, I know. But we got so much done this week. Everyone pitched in . . . got jobs."

After Selene and Tyler had moved out of their extra room, Halsey had gone to work in the school cafeteria and Sun Dog hired on with a landscape crew for the city.

"First my—our—room, now this," Selene said.

Lake lifted her spoon to her mouth, but she couldn't take another bite. Selene had only pretended the move was okay. Nothing had really changed. She had seen the look on Selene's face, the look she had tried to hide on the moving day. It was all just pretend.

"Besides, Selene," Ty was saying, "it's only temporary."

"Tyler." Selene's voice turned thick and low. "It isn't just temporary. It's fifteen years. Fifteen years of this. Still nothing . . . of our own." The next words came out like a cry. "You get your dream at my expense."

Lake stared at the bowl of beans in her cupped hands. How had Selene known what she was thinking? How could her own thoughts come out of Selene's mouth?

"Don't look at me like that," Selene said, and even if Lake was out in the barn and her parents were inside the house, she knew exactly the look Selene meant. It was as if Selene, not Ty, had failed.

"Don't look at me. I'm sorry. Really sorry. It just isn't working for me . . . not any more."

Somebody's spoon clinked against a bowl, birds chattered low above them as they all sat there, on bales of hay or on the ground, and listened. No one moved to help the children as they usually did. And then Ty began his speech, the one they had all heard so many times. The speech about what they were doing here, how important it was to the world. About how Barataria had lasted longer than most communal experiments these days.

"We can't sell out. We're thinking in one-hundred-year segments, here. We let too many people down if we take the short route."

He went on and on about how they had to believe in their ideals and work and begin the world again.

"If we just talk things out," he said. "If we are dedicated and patient . . . Can't we just talk?"

"Talk, talk, talk. Every conversation," Selene said, "every damn conversation we have, you turn political on me. I fall all over your words. You trip me up. Well, it's all too . . . global."

"It's in your head, Selene. You can cope with anything if you get straight in your head."

The back door opened and Selene stepped outside. She closed the door quietly this time, just shut it tight and didn't look back as she walked toward the washhouse.

"Why don't we take a truckload of wood into town?" Andy said as he washed the soup bowls.

"Okay," Tyler said. Selene had disappeared into the washhouse. "Sure," he said as if he were thinking something else. And then louder, "Can we load it before time to pick up Sun Dog in town? Try to sell it today?"

48

Andy said why not, so it was decided. Everyone went back to the jobs they had volunteered to do, and Lake said she would help Ty and Andy. While Andy and Ty piled older, dry wood into the pickup, Lake agreed to split hickory logs for their own woodpile. Stockpiling wood was one of the winter jobs that everyone worked at, and even now in spring it was vital to store up enough wood for next winter.

Remembering what Ty had said about the pent-up energy released when the heart of the wood was revealed, she wrestled a big hickory log onto its end and tapped a metal wedge into its heart. Raising the ax high over her shoulder, she let it fall onto the wedge. She loved the ring of the ax, the crack and tumble of the log as it split open, the energy she released from her own body. She knew this log had not come from one of Ty's special trees. He called trees "cousin" and assigned one to each person—your own hugging tree, he said. He'd learned about the special kinship people could have with trees from Indians who were his teachers in an early commune in California. Lake's special tree was an oak in the back fields, and she often went there to wrap her arms around it, to feel its rough strength, to let the bark make a jagged dent in her cheek. Sometimes it felt like holding a real person, sensual, even sexual.

Ty picked up a dry hickory log and underhanded it up to Andy, who stood in the bed of the pickup, now almost filled with logs.

"Hey, Ty." Lake put down the ax. "You about ready to take off? I'm going in with you."

"Yes, we're ready. No, you're not going. No room. Sorry," Ty said over his shoulder as he threw another log.

"I'm going," she said. "People want stuff mailed. I'll get the mail—wait. Okay?"

She ran into the house and picked up the mail from Lana's desk while Ty and Andy threw an old tarp over the wood and tied it down.

"I'll ride in back. I'm going," she said.

"You can't ride back there. It's too full," Ty said.

"I won't fall off," she said, and when Ty grimaced, she added, "Okay, okay. I'll ride up here with you guys."

Lake slid across the seat close to Tyler, felt the melting warmth of the leather against her legs, the waves of heat coming off the windshield.

"We have to pick up Halsey and Sun Dog. There's no room, Lakey," Ty said. "Go on. Out."

He leaned against Lake and pushed her toward the open door with his shoulder.

"Wait a second!" She felt herself slide across the wide seat. "You're selling the wood, right? I can ride home in the back."

Just in time, Andy hauled himself up into the truck and slammed the door. Crushed between the two men, Lake caught the odor of sawdust and wet wool and barns.

"Let her go," Andy said.

"Never," Ty said, but he shifted the truck into reverse.

"Yeah," Andy said, pulling on his beard. He looked down at her. "She can sit on Sun Dog's lap coming home."

"Ha," Lake said, but a queer shiver fingered up her back and she couldn't look at Ty or Andy.

The truck engine turned over the first time Ty tried it, and Lake remembered how Sun Dog had tinkered with it the day before.

Bumping along the gravel road, sandwiched between the two men, sawdust on their shoulders and arms clinging to them like sand, she thought about being this close to Sun

50

Dog, maybe even sitting on his lap. She imagined how his arm might feel around her. Would she lean back against him or sit up straight with her hands firm and flat on the dashboard? She tried this now, sat up straight and away from her father and Andy, not touching either one. She watched the road disappear beneath their wheels, heard the change in sound from gravel to smooth, paved road. By the time they got to town, Lake had forgotten about Sun Dog. She was thinking about Vernelle Fox and maybe getting a job.

Now Tyler steered the truck into a narrow space between two cars, parked at an angle in front of the post office.

"You want to run in?" he said. "Mail that stuff?"

Lake slipped the letters into the blue box on the sidewalk and then ran up the flight of cement steps into the lobby. She picked up the farm mail from Mr. Leonard at the general delivery window. There were the usual letters marked "Please Forward" or "Not Here" across the front, addresses scratched out and new ones added. Only the USDA Farm Bulletins and Ty's letters from magazine editors were sent directly to Barataria Farm, Shellerton Forge, Kentucky. Mixed in with all the local throwaway junk, there was one envelope addressed to Selene. It was mailed from Nashville and came from Margo, Selene's friend from Barataria's early days. Lake walked around to the driver's side of the truck and handed Tyler the mail. He held Margo's letter up to the sun, peering at the green ink, the energetic, curlicued handwriting.

"That's Selene's," Lake said, slapping at him. When she tried to grab the letter away, he swung it up out of her reach.

"Don't worry about it, Lake," Ty said, without smiling.

"You act like I'm censoring her mail, right? Right, Andy?" he said.

Lake shrugged her shoulders, raised both hands, fingers outspread.

"Just teasing," she said. "It's a joke, Ty. A joke."

Or was she just teasing? There was something to worry about with Selene. Ty knew it. He'd heard Selene this morning. He must have put two and two together by now. It wasn't just their fight this morning. He must have noticed the way Selene stared out the window and didn't come to meals and didn't sit at her looms and sing way into the night. He put the letter on the seat beside him.

"Old rebel Margo, eh? Wonder what's happening with her?" Tyler spoke to Andy. "Remember when Margo and . . . and Selene used to do their music?"

Both men stared at the letter on the seat beside them as if it were a person alive and they were waiting for it to speak to them. Lake couldn't hear any more of what Ty was remembering. Then he shifted into reverse and looked out the rearview mirror.

"I'll pick you up in an hour, two hours," he said to Lake. "We have to dump this wood and then we'll be back. Find Sun Dog and tell him. Tell him one hour or so, right here, okay? In front of the P.O."

Ty poked his head out of the window and looked up, shading his eyes from the sun. "It's two, two-thirty. Tell him make it three-thirty, four, around there," he said as if he had never seen the letter with its green-inked words "Selene Moon Woman Gillespie" on the front.

Andy rolled his window down.

"Don't worry about Halsey. We'll pick her up."

"Where is he? Sun Dog?" Lake said as they pulled away from the curb.

52

Andy leaned out of the truck window, over his elbow, "Main Street," he hollered. "By those big planters near the bus station. . . ." He jerked his thumb toward the center of town. "And Lake, if you think you want a job, get one," he said. And they were gone, clattering up the street with their battered truck and the load of hickory wood.

7

Hurrying around the corner to the drugstore owned by Vernelle's father, Lake pushed into light so different from the yellowy glow of kerosene lamps she was used to that she stood for a moment, blinking. In the four or five weeks since she'd been there, she'd almost forgotten the hiss and crackle of the fluorescent lights above her, making everything cold and blue. Inside a telephone rang over and over, a cash register whirred open, and there was a murmur of voices. She headed straight for the soda fountain in back where Vernelle might be working. What she wanted more than anything was a chance to tell her about Sun Dog, about Selene, and maybe ask her about a job there.

Besides, Lake had to admit, she was curious. She wanted to see if Vernelle's eyebrows had grown back. Vernelle had shaved them off right down to the bone a week before school was out. She did it because Mr. Fox wouldn't let her ride to Hopkinsville with a carload of boys to a baseball game. She lathered on Ivory soap and shaved off every last hair with her mother's pink-handled razor. Mr. Fox had grounded Vernelle for three weeks. At the time Lake wondered what would happen if *she* shaved off *her* eyebrows.

Actually she knew what would happen. Ty and Selene and all the others would say, "We understand. We wonder about your ego strength, Lake, but we understand." And then they'd tell stories about how their parents couldn't deal with long hair and beads. Or maybe they'd give her a big group hug. Or maybe they wouldn't even notice.

But Vernelle was grounded and, what was worse, she still had to take the consequences and come to school looking that way. Boys, including Kesey, made bets on whether her eyebrows would grow back or not. No one could look at her straight because they saw exactly what she would look like dead. She looked so . . . naked, somehow.

"Hey, Lake. It's ESP! I've been thinking about you all day long. What's going on?" Vernelle said when Lake sat down on one of the stools. She reached across the marble counter and took Lake's hand in her bony hand.

"I've been wishing I'd get to see you," she said. "I wish to heaven you had a phone. There's something I really, really have to tell you. And it is ser-i-ous," she said.

Vernelle always had something, some little secret she just had to tell. It was one of her specialties. She acted as if you were the only person alive and she needed to see you right that second, life or death. That's why she was best friends with townies and farm kids and even counterculture kids. She hugged and patted you, pulled you into her circle—her aura, Lana would have said. But the secret she wanted to tell, if it was truly a secret, was probably nothing. Still, even if it was just some whispered gossip about a boy, Kesey maybe, Lake was curious and flattered.

"Well, here I am then. Hi," Lake said, looking hard at Vernelle's eyebrows. Leaning as far as she could over the sink and stacks of dishes, Vernelle offered up her face as if it were a picture on a wall to be looked at but not claimed. She smelled like perfume samples.

"Not growing back," she said, pressing her lips together. "You know, I don't know what in the world possessed me." She ran her fingers over the bony promontory above her eyes. "Well," she said, "I'm not going to think about it anymore. What's done's done."

She brushed her wispy bangs back and wriggled what used to be her eyebrows up and down. The light brown, drawn-on eyebrows moved, too. "You like these?" she said. "I copied 'em out of *Ms* magazine. April issue."

"They're nice. They're okay," Lake said. One was lower than the other and Vernelle looked a little lopsided.

Every time Lake came into the drugstore, Vernelle wanted to fix her an extra-large hot fudge sundae. Although Lake never had any money to spend, Vernelle didn't care. She nearly always had money to lend or even give away. And if it wasn't money, it was gifts from the drugstore. "Come on, what do you want?" she would say. But mostly it was the sundaes she made, sundaes for all her friends and she never told her father about it.

Vernelle lifted a chrome dish from the stack of sundae dishes and propped open the folding glass door above the cartons of ice cream. Up to the elbow in cold vapor, her white arm disappeared into a deep well of chocolate. With red-tipped fingers she pushed the ice cream off the scoop and into the dish. As she ladled a dark river of chocolate over the ice cream, she licked her fingers.

"Nuts?" she said, and before Lake could answer, she sprinkled on a spoonful.

"We don't have stuff like this at the farm," Lake said.

"Yeah, yeah. You told me. Chemicals, right?" Vernelle spooned out a big bite of ice cream, ate it, and handed

56

Lake the long-handled spoon. Lake let the ice cream and chocolate sauce slide down her throat.

"Contraband!" she said.

The only junk food they ever had on the farm was a bottle of soda once in a while or packages of Oreos or gingersnaps Andy sneaked into the house.

She ate it all, licked the spoon until Vernelle said, "You can't lick that thing any cleaner."

"What were you going to tell me?" Lake said.

"Lake, remember that parent-teacher meeting? Last March or April, maybe? That old man that got up . . . said all that stuff about your family?" Vernelle twisted a strand of her long red hair. "Old Man Simon it was. He's on the school board? He called you all . . . called you names and things? Communists and . . . He said you ought to go somewhere else to school?"

Lake remembered all right. How could she forget? There was a woman, too, the mother of one of her friends. She had said, "Let 'em teach their own. Let 'em take their commie ideas back to . . . New York or some such a place as that. Take all their chanting with 'em."

A few people in the audience had stood up and said the Barataria people were fine just as they were, good neighbors—keeping stewardship over the land, they'd said. Others had applauded. But Lake would never forget the names and the look of hatred on Mr. Simon's face.

"Lake." Vernelle looked down at her red, pointed fingernails clutching the marble counter, "Those old people are figuring a way to put you in another school district. Move you out of Shellerton Forge Schools."

"How, I'd like to know. We already go here to school. It's all legal. The Van Emmerlines went to school here years back." She couldn't look at Vernelle.

57

"It's something about redistricting, redrawing the school boundaries? Making new lines. I heard my daddy say Barataria isn't really in Shellerton Forge Consolidated Schools anyway. Never was legally. Somebody just made a special temporary deal way back then, forty years ago, for the Van Emmerlines."

Lake couldn't sit there any longer. She had to tell Tyler. She felt as if everyone in town, everyone in the drugstore or walking by on the sidewalk, was staring at her, thinking she was part of the farm and all the things people hated. She couldn't imagine why, after five years of being part of the community, after five years of Ty's work with their neighbors, this had happened.

If Barataria kids couldn't go to Shellerton schools, they would have to ride a school bus for an hour or more each way, she knew. And she was sure Ty would never let them ride a bus when they could walk. He would say that an hour's ride on the bus carried them too far away from the work they had to do. She remembered how Kesey had had to quit football to help get up the hay.

Vernelle was still talking, asking what will you do and saying gee, I'm sorry and people are really sick and not everyone feels that way.

"Don't worry about it," Lake said. "We can always do what we've done before." She stood up and tucked her T-shirt into her jeans. "We can go to school right on the farm. Selene . . . my mother and father and some of the others can teach us. We've done that before. Don't you worry about a thing."

"Wait, Lake. I got something else. You aren't going to like it one bit . . . I hate to tell you this, but . . . Lake? Did you-all really dance around your yard . . . totally naked? Naked?"

"So? So what if we did? We didn't hurt . . ."

"Someone saw you." Vernelle peered at Lake from beneath her drawn-on eyebrows. "Lake, were you-all really . . . bare naked?"

Lake felt cold. Now she remembered the two trucks driving slowly past the farm the night they painted the Children's House. She didn't want to look at Vernelle a minute more; Vernelle with her bony face and her fake eyebrows, her generosity, and the way she took everyone in, belonged everywhere. Even Tyler, Tyler Gillespie IV, who grew up belonging everywhere he went, didn't belong here, not anymore. She had to get away from Vernelle and everybody in town. She twirled around on the stool and stepped down carefully, as if it were just any old day and not the end of the world.

"Listen, I have to go. I have to, uh, pick up some people."

"Wait a second. You're not mad, are you? What are you going to do? Do you want me to . . ."

"No," Lake said. "You don't have to do anything. I have to leave."

She moved down the aisle, past Vernelle who stood there behind the counter, her bony hand with the polished fingernails raised in a weak little wave. She was just like the rest of the people in town—looking down on anyone who wasn't just like them. Lake could hardly wait to get back to the post office to meet Halsey and Sun Dog and Ty and Andy. She hurried out of the drugstore as the lights on the funeral home blinked on. The neon sign shook itself in the twilight. Then it stayed lit, casting blue light onto the ground. Lake ran down the street without looking back at Vernelle. She hadn't asked her for a job and now she knew she never would.

59

8

Lake ran up a side street away from the drugstore and didn't look back to see if Vernelle might be following. She couldn't think about Vernelle or about looking for Sun Dog now. All she could think about was that next year she was supposed to graduate from Shellerton Forge. Would the new school accept her home teaching credits? And what would happen now to her dream of going to college? Even though there was no money, she had hoped for a scholarship. Some of her teachers encouraged her and told her she could work for some of the cost. When she told Ty and Selene about her dream, they worried, but agreed. But now everything was changed. New teachers at a new school wouldn't know anything about her qualifications. She'd have to start all over.

She was out of breath and sweating. She'd have to get to the post office quickly to tell Tyler and Andy about Vernelle's gossip. No, she worried, it wasn't gossip, it was real. She tried to imagine how Ty and Selene and maybe Free might stand up at the school board meeting and convince everyone not to change the districting. But the picture in her mind was blotted out by the memory of the painted house and the way they all had hung their paint-spattered clothes on trees. Slowing down, she leaned against the warm brick wall of the furniture store and breathed in deeply. She told herself not to worry. Vernelle tried to look important, sometimes pretending to know things no one else knew. It wasn't time to worry yet, she reminded herself. Besides, she had to find Sun Dog.

When she found him, just as Andy said, Sun Dog was on Main Street near the courthouse standing close to the back end of a city truck. He had a flat of blue ageratum in his arms. Wearing his black hat tilted off his forehead at a queer angle, he chewed on a toothpick as if he were trying to get even with it for something. Caked with black dirt, his hands moved in the blue flowers. His clothes were mud-spattered and his hair looked rough and dirty, not silky as it usually did. If she hadn't known him, Lake realized, she would think that he was a loser, somebody coming down from a bad trip. She stared at his knees, bare and dirty through the holes in his jeans. Lake couldn't give him Ty's message now. She couldn't let anyone see her talking to him.

She ducked into the doorway of a dress shop, pressed herself close to the glass display window. That was it, he looked like a burned-out hippie. It was as if he had never existed in any way but this; she couldn't picture him all silver in the blue moon, his fringed hair and the blue paint in his hand, smiling at everyone in meeting. He crawled on his hands and knees, half in the street, half on the sidewalk now, and as he sidled along, he troweled out little holes in the dirt of the flower box. Picking up a tiny plant, he tucked it into the earth, and Lake didn't want to notice that he did it in the same gentle way he tucked Halsey's baby into her basket. He wore the same soiled T-shirt with VER-

ITAS printed on the front that he'd worn that first day. When he rubbed his hands across his chest, she heard him say, to no one in particular, "I am rubbing out the old truth."

Lake wanted to turn away. She didn't understand her own feelings about Sun Dog until she remembered the first time Selene and Ty had come into her classroom here in Shellerton Forge. They had come for teachers' conferences and big rough-looking Andy came with them. Ty and Andy were the only men in the room. Except for Selene, who wore a striped wool vest knitted for Andy from everybody's leftover yarns, they wore their farm clothes. The vest was too big for Selene and one shoulder slipped down over her bare brown arm. All the other mothers wore silk blouses and plain sweaters, sheer panty hose and heels, not sandals and thick homemade socks. While their hair was cut short and permed, Selene's wiry hair straggled down her back, held back with a red rubber band. It was shame Lake felt at that school visit, for her parents and for herself. Now she had that feeling again and she didn't like it. All she could do was to try to focus on the store window filled with mannequins wearing bright bathing suits and cover-ups.

Then Mr. Fox and Bill Willets, wearing identical suits and white shirts and striped ties, came out of the bank together. Mr. Willets was the loan officer who had turned down Ty's loan application during the drought last year and, Lake remembered, was elected to the school board in November. They walked past her toward the cement planter boxes where Sun Dog still worked. When they stopped to talk, they stood close enough to Sun Dog to touch him as he knelt on the sidewalk. He might as well have been a fire hydrant, for all the attention they paid him. But he saw them, all right, Lake was sure of that.

Still down on his hands and knees, he edged closer and closer to them, digging, planting, pressing the black wet earth with his long graceful fingers. When he came close enough to reach them, without a change in his rhythm, surreptitiously Sun Dog stuck a little seedling into the cuff of each man's trousers. Lake expected one of them to notice—stop, bend down, look aghast, something. But the two men were so engrossed in their conversation they didn't notice when Sun Dog, quick and supple as a pickpocket, artfully gave each of them one of the city's plants. Still talking, they moved along the sidewalk as the tiny blue ageratum bounced and nodded and globs of wet black potting soil clung to their shoes. Lake gasped and covered her mouth with both hands to stifle the laughter that burst out of her.

When she could look again, Sun Dog was bent over the drinking fountain on the corner, washing his hands, splashing water on his face and beard. Water splashed out onto the street and people stepped around him to keep from getting wet. He didn't seem to notice them. There was a flower tucked behind each ear, blooming out of the dark earth of his hair. When he saw her watching him and laughing, he bowed low to her as if she were the queen of England. Of course he had known she was there all along, she thought. He did all that crazy, risky planting business because she was there watching him.

Farther up the street Mr. Fox and the banker were stopped by a third man, who pointed to their shoes, the blue flowers, their mud-soaked pants. Pointing, they looked back at Sun Dog, busy at the back of the truck. They retrieved a newspaper from a litter can and busied themselves cleaning off their shoes, while the third man, someone Lake had never seen before, ran toward Sun Dog, yelling curses. She hurried inside the dress shop, wishing she could disappear forever.

From inside the store she couldn't see what happened next. She waited for the sheriff's car to squeal around the corner, drive up fast, and park across the curb at an angle, expected to see Sun Dog pressed face down into the sidewalk, arms handcuffed behind his back or to the car door while the sheriff frisked him. But no sirens screamed, no police came. Sun Dog had disappeared.

"How come you came to town?" he was saying, smiling with his moist, glittery brown eyes, like a bird's eyes.

She had started walking toward the post office; she had decided to wait for Ty there, to tell him everything.

"You're crazy, you know that?" she said. She couldn't help staring at the silver drops of water clinging to his dark hair and beard.

"Sure I'm crazy. Aren't we all?" he said, and his eyes went blank for a moment. They walked along silent, not touching.

"You gonna be my ride back home?" he said. "Come to carry me away from this pain and sorrow?" he said, and put his arm around Lake.

Lake couldn't make up her mind whether to shrug out of his embrace or stay there and walk along with him, feeling the weight of his arm across her shoulders. But she didn't move away, she could only feel how her shoulder fit into his side and how his hand curved around her shoulder. Sun Dog sang under his breath, and she let him lead her almost as if they were dancing together to the music in his head, and she didn't care who might see.

*　　*　　*

At the post office Ty and Andy were waiting in the truck. Still wearing her school cafeteria uniform, Halsey sat between them. Andy jerked his thumb toward the back of the truck, and Sun Dog and Lake climbed in. Lake leaned against the cab and turned to look through the window at them. They were smiling as Halsey held up her dishwater-wrinkled hands. Everything seemed changed now. Lake's feelings of shame and embarrassment were gone. Even Sun Dog looked like himself again somehow—real, with some kind of beauty that Lake couldn't explain. From inside the cab Ty blew her a kiss and put the truck in gear for the drive home. It was beginning to get dark now, and as they picked up speed the cold wind surrounded her and rain began.

"It's cold," Lake yelled over the sound of the engine pulling up the steep hill out of town.

Sun Dog pulled the heavy tarp which had covered the load of wood up around them like a tent.

"Duck down here with me, green-eyed lady," he said, and something else, but those words were lost in the wind.

Everything smelled of fresh air and fresh-cut wood and plowed earth. Lake couldn't imagine why she'd been so ashamed of Sun Dog. She couldn't wait to get back to the farm, to sit around the big round table, eat and laugh, tell the family about where Sun Dog planted the ageratum. She pushed thoughts of school out of her mind. She didn't want to tell everyone about that. Not yet. She curled down behind the tarp, out of the wind and into Sun Dog's arms and the songs he sang to her.

9

Lake knew she had to tell someone about the school board's plans and maybe even about how mad Mr. Fox had been. But she couldn't decide whether to tell anyone about her feelings for Sun Dog. Somehow telling about the way she felt made it all seem real and set, like a bowl of Jell-O, and it was too soon for that, she thought.

She went looking for Selene or Ty. Ty was nowhere to be seen, and Andy said he might have gone back into town, he didn't really know. Selene wasn't in the washhouse or in the kitchen, so Lake headed toward the river, where Selene often went at dusk to meditate. At the riverbank near the back pasture Lake stepped onto the swinging bridge. The bridge skittered away from her, rocked and swayed as if it were a canoe.

Andy had been the one to build the bridge, something he'd learned in Vietnam, she supposed. His bridge was made of heavy rope and cedar, darkened now by weather. Some of the floorboards were missing. When they were younger, Kesey and Chad and children who had moved on long ago played a game, pretended to fall through the gaps and be swept away. They took turns hanging from the bridge by their hands, swinging like living pendulums. Back then the game felt like stepping off the safe edge of the world without wondering what would happen next.

She bent her knees and bounced a couple of times. The bridge threw her into the air and she came down again on both feet. She leaped from one board to the next, feeling the spring and sway, the rise and fall of the bridge beneath her feet. Below the shallow water rolled clean and brown over the sandy bottom of the river.

Selene was sitting on the flat rocky place beneath a big oak tree. Lake suddenly felt shy, reluctant to talk to anyone, least of all her mother. Her parents always said she could talk to them or anyone on the farm about love or sex or anything at all. What held her back now that there was something really important to talk over? She turned back.

"Hey!" It was Selene.

"Hey, yourself," Lake said. Holding on to the rope handrail, Lake let the bridge take her up and down, more and more slowly.

"Come on down."

"Well, I don't want . . . It's okay? You don't mind?"

"Heck, no," Selene said, and stood up to stretch with both hands at the small of her back. "Come on down."

When Lake settled down on the rocky platform hanging out over the river, she saw the letter from Margo in her mother's lap.

"Margo?" she said, and brushed her hands together, brushing off bits of earth and leaves and twigs.

"Yes."

Lake remembered little about Margo, only that she was tall and that her gypsylike clothes always smelled of marijuana. Margo had left Barataria six or seven years before and had a regular job now in the regular world.

67

"How did you know her?"

"Oh, we were in San Francisco—the Haight—together."

Selene smiled and threw a stick into the river. They watched it travel down the middle of the stream, turning around stones and roots.

"How come she's writing after all this time?"

"No special reason," Selene said.

But Lake knew by the look on Selene's face that it was special.

"Anything you can share?" Lake said.

"Sure, oh sure." Selene handed the folded page to Lake and leaned against the smooth tree limb that formed the natural seating on the riverbank.

"I didn't mean . . ." Lake said. The letter in her hand seemed to take the shape of a door into her mother's life and she didn't want to open it.

"No, go ahead. I want you to. Read it."

Dear Old Friend Moon Woman—Selene,

When you chose that name, you were just as weird as the people calling themselves and their kids Moon Unit and Prime Number and Dweezil and Woodstock, weren't you? If you come here to Nashville the way you ought to have done a long time ago, you'll have to go back to Eliza, sounds so much more country.

Speaking of country: Are you still into
    the earth-mother business these days?
How many quarts of peach preserves did you put up? And how fast did they eat them this year?
    Did the jelly even get jelled?
    Before they ate it all up?

Do you recall the year we did grape juice from all those grapes we picked wild and purple? We boiled every one of those little
PURPLE
things and strained them through cheesecloth bags we hung from a hook on the back porch with all the fruit flies clinging to it as if it was a lifeboat?

And then we bottled it?

Remember how it fermented down there in the cellar and how we lay awake all night long laughing and listening to those fool corks blow, bottles rolling
and
the juice splashing all over the floor? You've got to admit, even Tyler Gillespie—how come he never took another name like you did? Anyhow, Ty, send
HIM
my love and anything else he'd like from me just
ONE
more time. He laughed too that night. And then we got up and smoked some and drank some of that fermented juice and danced and loved and has us a real time. Remember? WOW!

Well, I hope you are doing your own life the way you want to. Be careful about who pays the bill— don't let it all be at your expense, sister.
    You always told me be CAREFUL
    what you ask for, you could get it!

                                    Love,
                                    Margo

Tucked inside the letter was Margo's business card, which gave the name of an advertising company and said she was an account executive. She had three phone numbers.

"There's more," Selene handed Lake another piece of paper.

Sun flicked in and out of leaves as Lake read, making the paper so bright she had to shut her eyes. Or was it the message that blinded her instead of sunshine?

Margo had written: ". . . I've told you this before. With your voice, old friend, you could sing backup for anybody. Maybe even solo, who knows? And right now, I repeat, NOW—I need someone to sing backup for a commercial I'm doing. You've got the voice for it. And, remember, you got a friend. So, if you still . . . Oh hell, call. You got a friend. And you got a job."

The door into her mother's life opened wider now. Lake glimpsed rooms and people and feelings and dreams that were not going to go away. It was as if she had come in and found Selene making love with someone. . . . She rubbed her face to make it go away. Tears came to her eyes again. She tried to feel the happiness Selene must be feeling; if she wanted it, there was a real singing job for her at long last. And if it was her dream, she ought to make it come true. Wasn't that what they all talked about sitting neck deep in the river on hot days or around the dinner table or the fire? How to make your dreams come true? First know what they are and then make them come true?

But what would happen if Selene left? What would Tyler do? Tyler who lived so totally in his own life, in his own choices, as if he were in a tunnel and could see only the end that he had in mind. What would happen to the farm . . . all the work that Selene did? Who would take over the gardening, the canning? Lana and Halsey would never want to do what Selene did. Lake dared not even think about herself. What would she do? She gazed into the water as if an answer to all her questions might be printed on the moving page of the river.

"What're you going to do? You going?" Lake said. She took off her sandals and dangled one foot in the cold water, watching the ripples curl around her foot.

"I'm not sure."

"You're going. I can tell."

"Yes, I am, Lake. No—oh, I don't know, honest. It's hard . . ." Selene threw another stick into the river and it sailed on down the stream in a crooked, meandering path.

"You want to. You do, Selene." Lake said.

"Yeah. Yeah, I do want to . . . give it a try. Yes." Selene sighed and the sound was close to a sob, ragged, tired. Lake couldn't think of anything to say.

"Can you see what I'm saying?"

"I guess so," Lake said. "Sure, but I don't want to understand."

"Lakey . . ."

"Ty—he needs you, too. The farm and all that . . ."

"You, too? You need me, too?"

"Sure."

But Lake wasn't being honest with Selene, the way Selene was with Lake. Who would take Selene's place? No one else had thought of applying for food stamps when the big drought came. No one else picked those mason jars out of the town dump. Lake remembered her mother's pleasure in the rows of jars filled with beans and tomatoes and halves of perfect peaches, in the carrots and turnips and potatoes buried in a sawdust box in the cellar. Was that all

71

there was about Selene? Her work? Lake felt ashamed and selfish.

Selene stood up, folded the letter again, and stuck it in her skirt pocket. She held out a hand to Lake.

"You going back?" she said. "I'm on lunch, I think."

"You're going then, really going?" Lake said.

"Yes. I have to talk to Ty and Lana and everyone." Selene turned to go back up the embankment.

"A meeting," Lake said, hope rising in her like yeasty dough. Everyone would talk her out of leaving. Or would they?

"You coming?" Selene said over her shoulder.

"No. I was . . . No," Lake said.

Selene stopped at the top of the ridge, on the path now. "Can you understand, a little bit maybe?"

"I have to get used to it, Mom," Lake said. "You know, I need time."

"Yeah, okay. I know. The worst part is your birthday and I wouldn't be here."

"We never make anything of birthdays around here," Lake said.

It was true. Individual birthdays weren't celebrated. Individuals didn't count; it was the family, they decided, that should be celebrated. Still there was something about your sixteenth birthday that seemed special to Lake.

"I know." Selene didn't let go of the rope handrails and she didn't turn around. "But maybe we could . . . Don't you want to do something special this year?"

Lake didn't answer. She watched Selene and noticed the way she fought the swaying bridge, came down when it came up, wouldn't let it carry her.

"We'll talk later, okay?" Lake said.

72

She lay on her back, watching her mother cross the bridge. Looking into the canopy of leaves, she heard the complaints made by tree limbs as they scraped against each other. Her mother was gone, she'd disappeared into a thicket of green, and Lake hadn't said one word about the school thing and nothing about Sun Dog.

When the sun went behind a cloud she leaned against the tree, felt its strength on her back and decided she would not cry. She wouldn't cry ever again, but when a ladybug with her shiny red and black wings landed on her arm and Lake tried to sing:

> Ladybug, ladybug
> Fly away home
> Your house is on fire
> And your children are burning

she couldn't keep her promise to herself.

10

Lake tried to relax, to stop the thoughts about Selene. She curled up under a pile of quilts in her loft with *Zen and the Art of Motorcycle Maintenance.* Sun Dog had lent the book to her. Maybe the cross-country adventures of father and son would take her mind off Selene. She read without seeing the page, without understanding one word, seeing only a picture of her mother riding on the back of a big Harley Davidson, riding away from her. Something, some small sound made her put the book down and sit up.

The hollow-voiced redbones down in the barns barked wildly. They barked every night at every little 'possum twitch or chipmunk scurry, but when they were quiet again she heard the sound that had worried them. She knew exactly what it was and what it meant. Her heart lurched against her chest. It was unmistakable: car tires crunching against gravel. She threw the book onto the floor and hurried downstairs. She didn't take time to find her shoes, only to pull on a T-shirt and a pair of jeans.

The dark umbrella of sky was filled with gray clouds, still full of rain, though none fell except that which had already fallen onto leaves and then heavily, again, in the wind. The grass was cold and wet beneath her bare feet. Lake peered into the blackness but saw nothing, heard only the car press against the dark with no lights and no engine. She knew, oh, she knew what it was. She hurried, her palms sweating and her throat too full of her own heart to call out, hurried across the muddy yard toward the driveway. Even though she couldn't see it yet, she knew it was the old brown Fairlane. At the foot of the drive just before the climb uphill through the row of trees, the engine coughed, sputtered, and started.

Lake found the shortcut to the ridge road and scrabbled up the red clay embankment. Shivering and wet now, her T-shirt already cold and damp against her skin, the legs of her jeans wet and muddy, she stumbled out into the road. If only she were warm, she thought, rubbing her arms. She waited on the road for the car to come toward her. In her mind's eye she saw her parents kiss each other. She had seen them yesterday, a week ago, she couldn't remember.

They stood at the edge of the wood lot where they had been cutting black walnut and cherry to sell in town. Selene wore a red bandanna tied low across her forehead. Tyler carried a long, flexible weed stem in his hand. He twirled it round and round like a whirligig as they walked. The twirling went fast and then slowed and then Ty threw the stem like a javelin into the woods. They stopped in the shadow of leaves, and the sun flicked back and forth on their faces. And then, as if in a formal dance, they both stepped forward one step so the tops of their bodies barely touched. Lifting their arms as if they were marionettes on strings pulled by someone else, they touched cheeks and stepped back. It was as if they didn't know quite what to do next, like children in a school play on stage in front of their parents.

She heard the car whine, pull up the hill, and then turn onto the ridge road. The lights flashed on, and she heard the door slam shut. She stood in the center of the road, with her arms wrapped around herself.

"Stop, please, stop," Lake cried, blinded in the head-lights. She waved her arms like a school crossing guard or maybe someone on a railroad track with the noon train bearing down. The car lights went off but the car kept mov-ing, slowly now. Lake had to step back out of the way.

It was Selene. Of course it was Selene. Lake looked in at her mother and, through the shattered side window, Se-lene's face seemed broken like the Picasso woman's face in a picture in the art room at school. All broken, Lake thought.

"Lake, honey," Selene said out the half-opened window, "go on. Go on back. I left you a letter . . . I . . ."

"No." Lake shuddered and it was more than the cold. "No! You come on back."

"I can't."

"Yes, you can," Lake said, and finally she could touch the car. "Where are you going, anyway?"

"I told you. Nashville. You know what Margo said. Oh, don't ask me that," Selene said.

"You can't, you can't just leave, Mom," Lake said, and knew that word meant everything. "Why didn't you tell me? You told Ty. I saw you."

"Oh, God. I did tell you. At the river. You didn't want to . . . hear. Please—oh, don't do this to me, Lake. Please."

"To *you*?" Lake screamed now.

Selene put both hands on the steering wheel and leaned

against it. Her wiry dark hair fell across her face. This time Lake couldn't push that curtain back and look into her mother's eyes to see what was there.

"Lake, why can't you . . ."

"—to you? What about Ty? And—me?" and the *eeee* sound of "*me*" seemed to bloom and grow and keen off into the green woods above them.

"Lake." Selene opened the door. The overhead light flickered off and on above her. Selene leaned out of the open car door, the overhead lights inside shining on her head and on the torn seats and the dusty dashboard. She stretched out one hand to Lake.

"Don't," Lake said, and backed away. "Don't touch me."

"Please, honey, I need you to understand why." And she drew herself back into the car. "You said . . . I thought you understood."

Lake slammed the door and the sound reverberated along the rocky sides of the road. Her mother fell back into the darkness of the car.

"I understand, all right. I know why you're leaving."

Lake couldn't bear to say what she thought. If she never said the words out loud, then she wouldn't have to believe them.

"Oh, Lake," Selene said.

"Go on, then. Go on, get out of here. We don't . . ." Lake was crying now in great noisy sobs, gulping for air as if she would never be able to breathe again.

Selene tried to roll the window all the way down and the handle came off in her hand as it always did. She held it a long time, looking at it as if it were alive. And then she threw it out the window. It clattered on stones and landed in the ditch.

"Lake, you're going to be fine. And I will not . . ." Selene didn't finish her words. The key turned in the ignition and the car started on the first try. Maybe it was a sign for Selene. Lake didn't know anymore.

"Go on back, Lake. I'll write. And you know why I have to do this. I know you know."

Lake could only stand there in the middle of the road with her hands over her mouth. But when the car began to move faster and faster she stretched out her hand toward her mother.

"Mama! Mama!" she cried, following down the dark road after the car. She ran as long as she could, ran until a sharp pain in her side came so hard that she could not breathe. She fell to her knees in the dark in the gravel in the cold.

"The ceremony will commence at high noon on this day," *Noble Justice said. "Today is the most auspicious time for* *the consecration of the Cosmic Family as one being."*

There were two circles, one outer circle of grown-ups *and inside that a circle of children who were old enough to* *be given to Noble Justice. Ty told Lake over and over not to* *say it that way.*

"You are only becoming a part of a bigger family. The *Community," he told her.*

But Lake knew it was to Noble Justice she was being *given.*

The wind blew hard and hot, and the sun beat into her *head until her eyes watered for the brightness of it. Lake* *wore a rough dress made of bleached flour-sacking and a* *crown of purple asters and blue chicory woven by the older* *girls. They told her she would be the one to make tiaras* *next time they had the ceremony. All the children in the* *circle wore the same halo of flowers and they carried a single stalk of Queen Anne's lace. Lake looked deeply into the blossom to see the black dot in the center.*

"Don't you know, little lady, that's a bug in there?" Noble said. "It'll sting you, you don't be good and get your karma right."

Stiff-armed, she dropped the wilting flower.

Noble Justice stood in the center of the circles, his white beard swimming over his shoulder in the wind. He wore a yellow robe. At some signal that Lake didn't see or understand some of the older children stepped toward Noble, smiling, looking back over their shoulders at their parents. Accepting the flowers they handed to him, Noble spoke to each one in his deep, compelling voice. Lake waited, not knowing what she was supposed to do. Her friend, Annie Sky, beckoned to Lake.

"It's your turn, too; go on up there," she whispered.

Perspiration poured down Lake's sides under the thick cloth of her dress and she didn't move. She looked for Ty over her shoulder, but his face was hidden beneath his broad-brimmed hat. He wasn't looking at her, and she thought that this meant she didn't have to enter that other family. As Noble hugged each one, the children moved out and were taken into the larger circle of adults. The wind was as loud as a roar and full of fear. To Lake it was more frightening than the time one of their members and her son had died of the terrible fever they all had.

Noble stepped down from the platform the men had hammered out for him. He came toward Lake with his arms outstretched. Someone cried out. A terrible, high weeping broke the silence. Lake thought maybe it was Selene, but then she understood that it was her own voice she heard, keening into the hot sun and the waving sea of grass.

No one moved. Noble stood in front of her. His white beard stirred and his lips moved, lips as full and purple as if he'd been drinking grape Kool-Aid. Lake didn't hear what he said. She fell and rolled herself down the small rise of ground, and when she could she stood up and stumbled across a small bridge. She ran, not daring to look back. Her heart throbbed and her eyes and hands seemed to be full of blood, pounding. When would Ty get there, catch her up in his arms and fly with her, rise up into the sky with her? She waited for the sound of his boots on the wooden bridge. The only sound was Noble's voice calling her name. She looked back over her shoulder, searching for her parents. Ty was there with all the rest of Noble Justice's family, a stiff stick-figure on top of the hill watching as Noble tried to gather her into his family.

Ty was there, but Selene was gone. She had disappeared into the woods.

When she stood up, there was mud on her forehead, on her hands and knees. Lake snapped off a branch of serviceberry bush and wiped her hands and face with the leaves. Chilled by cold perspiration on her bare skin, she shivered and watched the car lights, no bigger than two candles, shine onto the valley road. They disappeared and then reappeared around curves in the road until finally the lights vanished for good into woods at the far end of the valley.

As she walked back to the house in the dark, she remembered that both Ty and Selene had finally rescued her, taken her away from the Cosmic Freedom Farm and Noble Justice's ideas. But all she could think about now was the long, the terrible long time she'd had to wait for them to decide to keep their family together.

11

A greenish light came through the three wide windows in the loft. Walls, floor, her sleeping bag—all seemed to have been painted with water. Lake hadn't slept all night waiting for the sound of Selene's car to come back down the lane, her footsteps to cross the gravel yard, the light to blink off in Ty's room. Of course the sounds never came and the light in the Big House was still visible. Selene was gone and that thought blotted out any other thoughts in Lake's mind. She lay for a moment listening to the birds calling and answering each other.

Selene was gone. All right, so what comes next? she thought. And then it came to her. This was her birthday, and even though yesterday she was fifteen and today she was sixteen with all that that meant, nothing about her had really changed. She was still the same tall heavy-thighed girl she'd been last night. Her face hadn't become heart-shaped overnight like Selene's. She held her sturdy, wide-palmed hands out in front of her now. They were the same: fingernails broken, slightly dirty, and nothing at all like Selene's long, narrow, and delicate hands. No, there was no change inside or out, she knew that, even while she hoped that her birthday would bring a new feeling inside, a new understanding of what it meant to be growing and alive.

Something reminded Lake that no matter what else had happened, she was on breakfast duty this morning. As she walked from the Children's House over to the kitchen, Lake wondered if Selene had driven toward Nashville all night. Would the mist hang in the low fields between the hills the way it did here? Did fingers of fog reach into the hollows where she was sleeping in some little motel or maybe still driving, driving?

When Lake came into the kitchen she let the screen door slam behind her. Selene was supposed to be there, cooking oatmeal, but only Free was there, stirring something in two big pots. Someone had already set the table on the back porch carefully; the bowls matched the plates and early spring wildflowers were arranged in a blue jar. Sun Dog, she thought. No one did that kind of thing around here except Sun Dog. Not even Selene.

"She take off last night?" Free said.

"Yeah," Lake said without looking at him.

"I guess she's gotta do what she's gotta do." Free held on to the wooden spoon as if it were a lifeline, peered at her through round metal-rimmed glasses.

"Right."

"We all saw it coming," he said. "Man, all those songs about leaving on a jet plane? Looking for a home?"

"She's got a home," Lake said. "And what are we supposed to do?"

"What can *we* do?" Free said. "It's her—"

"I mean about breakfast," she said, taking spoons out of the cabinet. Lake knew her eyes were still red from crying, but Free didn't seem to notice.

"Oatmeal's ready," he said. "I did it. She baked the bread yesterday, I guess."

Lake threw a loaf of Selene's dill-and-spice bread onto the wooden table and then stabbed a knife in it. The knife quivered, stuck upright in the table.

"I mean," she said, "what can we do about her?" She knew she was making no sense.

"Nothing." Free pulled the knife out and began to slice the bread, thick slices falling away from the knife like cards. He stacked them on a tray. "Nothing. That's what we can do." He looked at her more closely. "Does Ty know?"

Lake didn't answer. Of course Ty knew. His light was on all night, shining forlornly across the dirt yard.

Lake poured milk from the pail in the cooler into a yellow glass pitcher, which usually cast a circle of light onto the floor in the sun, but this morning the pitcher was closed and opaque.

"I guess Ty will have a lot to say about commitment, all his regular speeches. . . ," Free started.

"You don't have to listen," Lake said. "Why don't you just leave? Everyone else does. We're like a revolving door around here. Everybody comes. Everybody goes."

She felt half crazy, arguing with Free on both sides of the question when she knew he was as worried and sad as she was. They ladled oatmeal cereal into thick blue bowls and carried them to the side porch for the children.

Their hands on each other's shoulders, the children were marching around the yard in circles in time to a sing-songy chant.

Selene's gone.
Didn't pack.

Selene's gone
and she won't be back.

When Lake heard the words she slammed the pitcher onto the table, spilling milk on the floor. She pushed open the screen door and rushed out.

"Shut up. *Shut up!*" she yelled, waving her arms at them. "Damn you, oh damn you!"

Scattering like chickens, they kept up the rhythmic chant until Lake caught Chad, who screamed the chant even louder than before. Hearing Lake's shouted threats only persuaded the children to sing louder and louder.

She won't be ba-ack.
She won't be ba-ack.

Lake threw Chad to the ground. He stood up, lowered his head, and ran at her like a billy goat. He butted her in the stomach. She swatted at him, and when he tripped, Lake jumped on top of him and wrapped her legs around his skinny body. She put both hands over Chad's open mouth.

"Shut up. Shut your mouth," she cried.

When Chad bit her, Lake rolled over and over in the dust, holding her hand and cursing.

"Hey!" Andy rushed out of the barn only half dressed. "You kids," he said. "You know we don't cop to that behavior around here. Time out."

He picked Chad up and offered his T-shirt to wipe off the mud on his hands and knees. He took Lake and Chad by the arm.

"You first, Lake. What's happening here, man? Sounds pretty heavy."

Lake wiped her hand gingerly on her jeans and held it in

her other hand. "They're leaning on me," she said. "I'm not . . . Their damn cute little song." She brushed mud off her jeans.

"You guys know the rules," Andy said. "Settle it. But be quiet about it. Don't bother the rest of us with your junk."

As she ran across the yard toward the woods Lake heard the children complaining that their oatmeal was cold and the bread had a big hole in it.

Lake found Tyler in the small barn, working on the old Farm-all.

"Hi, kid," he said. "You don't look so red-hot."

A piece of cord dangled from his hand. "Short-wiring the Slouching Beast again," he said. "First we do the ignition and then the trans—oh, Lake."

He opened his arms. She stepped into them, afraid to look at him, really look at him.

"Bad news, eh?" he said with his face pressed against her hair.

She let him hold her, smelled diesel fuel and hot metal on his shirt and the perspiration.

"Why'd she have to go, Ty? Couldn't you guys work it out?"

"She has to do what's best for her now. That's what she says. It's her turn after all this time." Ty said this as if trying to convince himself, not Lake.

"I don't see . . ."

"It's just . . . you know how she sings. She wants to do something with it—she thinks she's getting too old. She talks about all the young ones. Emmylou Harris. Lacey somebody. Linda Ronstadt."

"Fine. Fine. But what about us?" Lake closed her eyes

and saw the farm all green and growing, saw how Ty's work was beginning to pay off.

"She's tired," Ty said, wiping his wrench off with a greasy rag.

"Tired, yeah. Tired of us."

"No. Come on, Lake. Tired of the farm, the work, the— this just isn't her dream anymore."

"In all the other communes, it's the animals that have to leave first," Lake said. "Not here . . ."

"Yeah, they get too expensive to keep," Ty said, staring off into space.

She looked past the barns, out toward the alfalfa field almost ready to show its blue blossoms, the big garden plowed and disked, radishes and lettuces showing in warm corners.

"What now?" Lake pulled tufts of stuffing from the tractor seat and let them fly as far as they would in the wind.

She remembered Ty's words about how the return of spring was a wonderful moment in life, how nothing ever really dies.

"She wants something more. Something of her own."

"She doesn't want us. That's for sure." Lake pressed her head against the steering wheel so hard that it hurt. She hoped it would make a red mark there that would never go away. This was worse than all those times they had had to run away, worse than the time Noble Justice had claimed her, worse than waiting for Ty and Selene to rescue her.

"She doesn't *have* us," Ty said. "We have only ourselves, and we're part of this big family here, Lake. You know how we feel about that."

"She had me, all right. She birthed me, Dad. Sixteen years ago today. Doesn't that mean anything?"

She hadn't meant to mention her birthday. But he didn't seem to notice.

"It means a lot. But it doesn't mean forever . . ."

Lake cried out, "She told me. She told me once. What about all that primal bonding she talks about? She said when you carry something around inside you for almost a year, you feel a lifetime attachment. But she lied."

"Oh, Lake, she still means every word of that. You know she does. Things'll be okay. I know you're worried. Scared maybe. I am. But . . ."

"Why can't we go with her? You and me? You did that once—that time we left Colorado. You had a farm there, too. Dad?"

"I'm not going to do that, kid." Ty took off his head scarf and wiped his face with it. "I've made a life here. I've worked too hard. When we create this farm we create our-selves, too. Lake," he said. "I want to stop roaming around. I want to think in one-hundred-year segments now. No more short-term stuff, picking up and . . ."

He pointed out toward the fields. "You don't remember what all this was like when we came here? Lifeless. Worn out. And now it . . . grows things, Lake. Sustains us."

Of course Lake did remember, but she could only ask, "What about her?"

"Lake." He was getting angry; she could see it. "All I know is it's her turn now. I don't have to like it, but that's the way it is. Don't push me anymore on this. I need some time, too."

He lay down on the creeper, pushed himself beneath the tractor. She put her hands around the steering wheel. Sud-denly, she was overcome with envy and longing that filled her eyes with hot tears; envy for the ordered and peaceful lives of people in the regular world, longing for a life like theirs—all planned out, neat and safe.

Leaning her head against the wheel, she peered through the spokes at Ty. Nothing showed but his legs. The rest of him had disappeared beneath the tractor. His voice was distant, muffled, and she thought he might be crying.

"We're going to be okay, kid. Stick with me."

Lake leaned over the edge of the tractor.

"Dad, Ty," she said. "You think she'll be okay? Selene, I mean?"

Tyler pushed himself out from under the tractor again and she was looking into his bright blue eyes. Sometimes, Selene had said, they could make you do things with your life before you even knew you were doing them. His face was upside down and she stared at the way his lips curled the wrong way when he spoke.

"Sure, Lakey." His lips moved backward. "And now, if you think you're okay about this for now, I should finish this."

"Yes." She nodded. "Well, sure, I guess," she said, and Ty disappeared beneath the tractor again.

She started out across the field alone, walking along the outer edge of the newly plowed ground, not really sure where she was going. From the shelter of a large brush pile she heard the low buzzing sound *om* before she saw who was humming. Someone was behind the brush pile meditating. She came closer to the sound, found Sun Dog lying on his back in a patch of long grasses. The humming stopped. When Lake stepped off the path into the high grass, Sun Dog sat up fast as if he had heard something to be afraid of.

"Don't come crying to me, girl," he said with his back to

her. "I'm not your mama. You're a grown girl now. You'll . . ."

"I'm not crying. I don't cry," she said. "I thought you had a job. So why aren't you working?"

He lay down on the grass again.

"I don't need no little men wearin' their daddy's three-piece suits telling me where I can plant what. I told 'em I didn't need no advice or their . . . job. Besides"—he stared off into the distance for a long moment and his voice changed from the self-mocking tone it usually carried—"nobody pins me down. I don't want anybody getting too close to me."

Lake didn't know what to say. They needed his town job and the paycheck. That was the whole idea.

"I thought you wanted to talk about Selene," he said at last. "You know I'm not the one made her go. She had the idea long before I . . . She just didn't know it."

"Ty said she needs her own life. Music and all that."

"You could say that."

Lake walked closer to him. The wind blew his beard away from his face like a fringe of dark silk. She saw the wide gap between his teeth when he smiled at her and wondered what it might prophesy. For a little while she would lie beside him in the grass, watching feathery seeds float above them like tiny parachutes. She wondered what was inside those little packages, where they would land, what life they would start. Maybe Selene was like those seed parachutes floating above them, filled with pos-sibilities. Would she grow and bloom in Nashville now, in the garden where she was planted now, the way the brightly colored poster in the Big House said you should?

"A person has got to be willing, you know," Sun Dog said softly.

"Selene's not willing to do it anymore—all the farm work and being an outsider every place," Lake said, remembering how the mothers at school stared at Selene's long hair, her sagging skirts with mandelas tied in, and her raw, sunburned, pioneer woman look.

"You got to let her go, got to let her go, got to let her go." Sun Dog crooned the words and somehow she felt the dark, taut thread inside her let go and swim away somewhere.

Finally she said, "Today's my birthday and I . . ." She closed her eyes. She didn't want him to see how much she cared about her birthday and about her mother. Behind her eyelids she saw the sun-circle floating white in the red sea of her eyes.

"Your birthday? For whicn one of your numerous lives? I always knew you were an old soul, girl, living close to Nirvana," he said.

Then all the feelings, all the words she'd been holding back bubbled out of her along with hot, sudden tears. She asked him why Selene had to leave on her birthday and told him how Tyler didn't even care. Between sobs she asked him, "Don't you think. . . ?"

"Naw, you know I don't think. I just know."

He turned his head in the grass to look at her. His brown eyes were liquid, melting, and when he breathed she smelled marijuana again. He wiped the tears off her face with the heel of his hand.

"You have so many cosmic expectations," he said. "Well, this time they came true." He sat up and pulled something out of his pocket. "I have made for you the best kind of birthday gift a green-eyed lady could ever want . . . unexpected."

As she lifted her hair, he fastened around her neck a necklace made of tiny silver coins.

"It's beautiful!" she said, fingering the flat silver circles that seemed to have come from some exotic country in Sun Dog's mind. "You really *made* this? Where did you get it? How did you know it was my birthday? What . . . How did. . . ?"

"Too many questions. Too many. Can't you just enjoy the moment in time, go along with the flowing river we're in now? Right now?" he said, his voice had changed, seemed far away now.

She turned to look at him, picked a fringy seed out of his hair. Why couldn't she do what he suggested, relax and enjoy this moment? And why didn't she want to fall in love with him?

12

Even though the necklace Sun Dog gave her caught in her hair and hung too heavily around her neck, Lake wore it as she weeded, thinned, and watered the small vegetable garden. She hadn't seen Sun Dog since her birthday, but his gift was the only way anyone had marked the day and she needed the outward sign of it.

Now, plucking bright yellow-green lettuce seedlings out of their places in the earth, Lake could finally think about something besides Selene and Sun Dog. She had to think about Vernelle and Mr. Fox and Mr. Willets and school now. Her senior year would begin in September. What would happen to her plans for college or anything else for her own future? Everything seemed out of reach, impossible now.

She remembered Ty's rage when he found out about the school board's decision. It was Halsey who broke the news. Lake hadn't been the one to tell him, after all. Halsey had overheard some teachers gossiping about it in the Court House Café. When she told Tyler, he had thrown a hammer through a window and then didn't come in to dinner that night.

The memory of his rage and her own confusion about what might happen next were so insistent now as she worked in the lettuces that Lake didn't see or hear the black car with the city's gold crest painted on the side door until someone honked the horn.

It was Mr. Fox and Mr. Willets. Tyler, Andy, and Lana, their coffee cooling in mugs on the rail, stood on the side porch watching them. The car stopped. The two men got out. Lake stood up and stretched with both hands against the small of her back. Picking up the wooden lug filled with lettuce, wilting now in the sun, she walked toward them.

It didn't take long. In fact it was over before Lake crossed the yard. Mr. Fox handed Ty a letter and stepped back without saying hello or how you getting along or anything. Ty opened the envelope and began to read. While Andy fished his glasses out of his shirt pocket and Lana leaned over Ty's shoulder, the two men got back into the car, pushed a button to roll up the windows, backedaround the yard, and drove away. No one had said a word.

"I guess this makes it official," Ty said now, his face blank, showing nothing of his anger.

"They think it's a done deal," Andy said. "But we sure as hell don't."

He went on when no one answered.

"They can't do this. They can't kick us out of our own school," he said. "Ain't this supposed to be a free country?"

He started to take a sip of coffee, but instead threw the coffee, mug and all, over the railing. Tyler didn't even seem to notice. His arms hung down at his sides like ropes, and Lake didn't understand why he was so quiet. She stepped closer to him, wanting to help somehow. Lana took the letter out of Ty's hands and read it again.

"We'll just go up to the next meeting, plead our case," she said. "We've got time before school starts, plenty of time."

"Right," Lake said, wanting her father to say *yes, yes, that's right, let's get with it here.*

"Yeah. Right. We go up there, we plead our case, they listen and everything's all fixed up. No harm done," Ty said instead. "In your dreams," he added, talking through his hands, rubbing them hard across his face.

"We'll write our own letter. We'll . . . do something," Lake said. "Petitions, something! Come on, Ty!"

Why didn't he shake his fist at Mr. Willets and Mr. Fox, vow revenge, do something? Where is the real Tyler, she thought, the one who's so articulate, so persuasive? Charismatic was what the weekenders, even people who stayed long enough to be full members, called Tyler. Watching him stand there with his hands covering his face, she felt a surge of something inside her, shame or anger maybe. First Selene and her letter and now Ty collapsing like a tired balloon in front of her. No, it was fear, fear she hadn't known since that time with Noble Justice. She wanted to shake Ty until his teeth rattled in his head. He had just stood there on the high windy hill in the hot sun back then, too. He hadn't helped her, not that day, anyway, not until much later, when it was almost too late. But in spite of all her hope Tyler still didn't move or speak. There was none of Lana's bravado, none of Andy's anger. He just stared open-mouthed as the car disappeared over the ridge on its way back to town. Lake had seen that look before. It was the time the drought ruined all their corn and wheat and they all had to apply for food stamps.

Inside the cool, dim kitchen, empty before the business of making lunch, Lake put her lettuce thinnings into cold water, soused them up and down to wash the black dirt off. Lana went back to her office. Lake watched Ty and Andy walk across the dirt yard, still rutted from all the rain they'd had. They passed the tiled silo and went into the alfalfa field, lying as open as a lake in the sun. Free was out there with Chad and Kesey already. They would all be out there working in the fields all day, past dark probably. The hollow sound of cow bells mixed with their distant voices. She imagined Andy saying, as he always did, "We got to till that wet field down there where the corn washed out."

Free would say, as he always did, "Andy, with all your shoulds and oughts, you sound a hell of a lot like my father." And Tyler saying they'd get to it after haying, for sure, any day now.

The sound of another car, kicking gravel into the fenders, clattered down the hill. She poured water from her cupped hands onto her face to cool her skin. Of course. She took a deep, cool breath. She knew it. It was Mr. Fox and the banker come back to say the school board had made a mistake. Naturally they would apologize, she could go to school in town, they all could. It was all a big mistake. Drying her face with a dish towel, she opened the screen door, held it ajar, and waited for the car to get down the hill. Now, she thought, I'll be with Vernelle and the others. I'll have all my regular teachers. I can try for some kind of college aid again. Best of all, Tyler would get his wish, no Barataria kid would ever ride the bus for two precious hours a day.

Sun bounced off a rack of lights clamped to the roof of the yellow car. It was not Mr. Willets or Vernelle's father at all. It was Bascambe Bailey, the sheriff with two last names, which told everyone that he was kin to the first two families to settle the county one hundred fifty years ago.

"Hey, Lake," he called out. "Anybody around? Ty or anybody? I got to talk to somebody down here."

The smell of lilacs in the heat was overwhelming, so strong Lake could taste it. Why did her tongue go dry and thick at the sight of the sheriff? She couldn't speak. She jerked her thumb toward the fields.

"Lord God, Lake. Way out there? I'm not goin' way out there, not in this godawful heat," Sheriff Bailey said.

He wiped sweat off his upper lip with his thumb. He turned off the ignition and for some reason the car engine kept chugging. The car bounced for a moment and then settled down.

"You're so much younger and prettier than I am. Run out there for me, will you? You be a good little lady."

He smiled and Lake noticed that he had a gap between his front teeth, like Sun Dog.

"Just take 'em the word. Tell 'em I got one of their boys up at the jail. Had him all night. Like to drove us crazy, too. Singin'. Can't sing worth . . ."

"It's no one from here?" Lake didn't mean for her words to come out like a question.

"Says he is." Sheriff Bailey read from a clipboard on the seat beside him. "You got a Albert Cabot Jamieson stayin' here?"

Lake finally could take a breath. The name sounded like a name in *Newsweek,* one of those magazines she read at the drugstore, waiting for Vernelle sometimes. It sounded like someone with a fancy house, a senator, maybe, from some small eastern state.

"No," she said. "No one. There isn't anyone like that here."

"Funny. His driver's license, Master Charge says that's his name. Calls hisself Sun Dog?"

Why wasn't she surprised? Somehow she knew it would be Sun Dog. She started out to get her father, straight out into the hot yellow face of the sun. She fingered the necklace Sun Dog gave her and the little coins were hot, burning her throat. She unfastened the chain and put it in her shorts pocket.

Everyone gathered around the sheriff's car, shielding their eyes from the bright sun reflected at them from the windshield as the radio squawked like crows on a gray morning. Sheriff Bailey finally got out of the car, put on his hat, and switched his gun holster to a different place on his hip. Ty and Free rocked back and forth on their heels, looked down at the ground.

"Two, three days of this dry wind, I reckon you'll be mowing."

"Looks like it," Ty said.

"Some nice hay-making weather coming along behind that cold front."

The sheriff was taking his time.

"See you got that mess of hickory sprouts about cleared out up on the road," he said as he polished the chrome spotlight with the back of his arm. "You spray 'em?"

"No," Ty said. "We hacked them out. The hard way."

"Yeah," Free said. "We got a new man. Works like a dog. Goes at 'em a strip at a time. Really works . . ."

"That ain't all he's been a'workin' at," the sheriff said, and Lake was glad he finally got to the point.

"Say what?" Andy said.

"I say we got him over to the jail. People all over town got complaints out on him," Sheriff Bailey said. He looked straight at Ty.

"You ain't had a freaked-out one like this for a long time, have you, Ty? Steals. . . ?" He stretched out the word and kind of leaned into it as if it were enough to hold him up. "Steals everything ain't nailed down."

"You have something definite in mind? I can deal with it if it's a concrete, specific problem you have." Ty folded his arms across his chest.

"Well, paint for one. Mack? Up at the Mans Hardware? Says he had paint out back, turned his back, and it floated off into thin air." He made a sound like wind blowing and grinned.

"A little paint? Come on," Ty said, but his face went pale for a moment. "That paint was old, used up."

He glanced over at the Children's House where some of the crazy quilt of color had already started to peel off.

"Now, that ain't what Mack says."

"You got something else?" Free said.

"Yeah, I got something else. You want to try car parts, washing machine parts? How about flowers? Looks like your Mr. Albert Jamieson's got his smell over everything in town ain't tied down."

Sheriff Bailey hitched up his Sam Brown belt, got back into the car, fastened his seat belt, took off his hat, and laid it on the seat beside him.

"You comin' down and bail Mr. Jamieson out? You're

98

going to have to if you want him to help you with your haying there." He started the car.

"Say, Ty, I almost forgot." The sheriff's good-old-boy neighborliness was gone now. "Ty? You might want to know that Ray Fox and Bill Willets have signed a complaint, too. Looks to me like if your man is such a good hand, he ought to know where the hell the city's flowers ought to be planted."

13

As certain as Sheriff Bailey's prediction, the hot dry weather held and everyone agreed the hay was ready to cut. They didn't own a mowing machine or have the money to hire their neighbors' mowing machines even if they had wanted to, so they would do it themselves as they always did. They'd use rakes and scythes and the work of everyone handy to get the hay in—the faster the better. Whether Sun Dog could get out of jail in time to help wasn't clear, but Free and Lana would pay his bail with Halsey's latest paycheck.

They decided that with or without Sun Dog, they'd meet in the blue-green field the next morning while dew was still on the grass.

"The heavier the grass, the cleaner the cut," Ty said. "It'll cut rather than bend."

It was five o'clock in the morning and still too dark to see except in the light cast on the field by the old tractor's headlights. There was something about the light, Lake thought, not just this morning but every morning, that reminded her of the light in her grandmother's church. In the beamy light the Barataria people and the weekenders who came to help talked together in low, hushed voices, church voices. As they made their quiet plans, steam from their coffee cups rose like ghosts in the morning air. To Lake there was something comforting about the dark silhouetted figures huddled together, led there by the ancient, timeless rule of seasons. She saw Ty, his arms akimbo, his fingers laced together resting on the top of his blond head.

"We'll take the rows north to south," he was saying. "Let's put the best mowers in the front."

"Right," Andy said. "I'm not getting in your way. You'll cut off my legs and leave me there on my knees."

Everybody laughed, and Ty wrapped his arm around Andy's neck.

"I might do that. You never can tell, man. So leave plenty of room between you and me," he said.

And then, "This isn't a contest, you know. Keep lots of room and don't make too wide a cut. Okay? Now. Who wants to start out mowing and who wants to fix lunch and who wants to turn the windrows and stuff?"

Lake volunteered to mow and later rake up the fresh green grass into little piles. Ty handed Lake a scythe and said, "You remember how to do this, right? Don't forget, the grass teaches you."

Holding the scythe in her hands, Lake took her place beside and a few feet behind Ty. She made one swipe at the timothy grass with their heavy, wobbling heads. The weight of the scythe and the awkwardness of the curved blade carried her around in a circle and she almost fell. She looked at the stand of grass she'd tried to cut. Nothing much had happened to the grass. Most of it had bounced back upright. What had fallen under her blade was cut high and she remembered Ty and Andy quoting the old saying "An inch at the bottom is worth ten at the top." She took another cut and then another. The blade took on a menacing look to her. She couldn't make her body do what she wanted it to and she knew she would never do anything as easily and gracefully as Ty, who by now had moved along his own row, away from Lake.

"Hey, Ty. Wait up," Lake said. "Hey!"

He stopped and leaned for a moment on the wooden handle of his scythe.

"Don't cut such a wide swath, Lakey," Ty hollered down the edge of the hay field.

"I think I forgot everything I ever learned," Lake hollered back. "It's been a whole year."

A thin fringe of light appeared above the horizon and somebody turned the tractor lights off. The scythe was heavy in her sweaty hands and her muscles already ached from her clumsy effort. Looking over her shoulder at the uneven stubble of uncut grass and weeds she'd left standing, she tried to relax and recall the steps to easy mowing. She shrugged her shoulders up and down a few times.

"You'll wear yourself out." Ty walked toward her. "We're going to be out here all day long, so try to cool it. A two-foot swath is no disgrace." Ty smiled.

"It's a remembered reflex, Lake," Ty was saying. He stood beside her. "See. Look, it's not a broom, honey. This way. Like this. Don't face the field. Hold the blade up, parallel to the ground. Let the grass fall beside you. I like the zen of this." He moved off down the row almost like a dancer. "See, like this," he sang back over his shoulder.

Watching Ty work, Lake could almost believe that he was the same old Ty, eager to be in the fields, happy with their communal life. It was as if the school board hadn't turned against them. It was as if Selene had not gone away. For a moment Lake pictured the way her mother looked last year, with a red bandanna tying her long hair away from her valentine face and the grass falling in whispers from her scythe. She tried hard to concentrate on the work, tried to block out all the dark thoughts about Selene. Maybe Margo's offer had been only a nightmare she'd had, maybe, maybe . . .

Lake worked on down the row, following Tyler. The blade snicked through the grass more easily now. Low rays of the rising sun painted the windows of their houses red and glinted off the curved metal blade in little explosions. Deeper into the field, away from her, stretched out in a staggered line across the timothy field, Ty and Andy, Free and Kesey, Lana and some of the weekenders walked in unison, swinging their scythes, singing as they went, cutting the hay. They wore long blue jeans, long-sleeved shirts with the sleeves buttoned at the wrist to keep out the dust and insects. With their blue shirts billowing in the light breeze and their long hair, Lake thought they looked like a thin, blue snake slithering through the grasses.

The longer she swept the scythe back and forth across the grass, the more she remembered. She remembered how to use her arms more than her body. She remembered to keep her head up, to stand erect but lean into the work just enough to keep from losing her balance. It was like dancing or skating or riding a bike. The more you thought about it, the harder it was. Finally all there was was the *swish, swish* of scythe through grass, and the sun on her shoulders, her mind empty as if cutting hay were a meditation. It wasn't like being a machine, she thought, it was that she *became* the grasses, *became* the blade and the sun

103

and the heavy perfume. It was as though her body and her mind were one.

She came to the end of the row, and before she turned the corner she stopped a moment to look back at her work. The green and juicy grass lay in little scraggly, uneven piles. Her row was a little ragged, but she had done it. She was proud of herself and understood more than ever before what Ty must feel about the land and their husbanding of it.

She breathed in the smell of green and growing things, the new-mown hay sweetness. It was hot now; sun poured over her head and sweat clouded the dark glasses she wore. She was itchy and hot. Even though she had tried hard to use the scythe properly, remembered the way Ty let his left elbow almost hit his backbone as his upper body swung around, she was tired. Keeping relaxed, she decided, was hard work. She stopped and lifted her long braid away from her neck. The braid hanging down her back seemed as heavy and thick as a snake. She heard a low whistle and then a voice.

"Hey, green-eyed lady."

It was Sun Dog. There he was behind the hedgerow that separated grass from pasture. Behind him oats showed dark green through the stubble of wheat. Her heart turned over and she felt her face grow even warmer. Perspiration ran down her sides and into the waistband of her shorts. Bits of grass and seeds clung to her sweaty legs, and she wished she had worn long pants and a long-sleeved shirt like the others. She wiped her face with her T-shirt.

"You're supposed to be in jail," she said. She kept working.

"Who, me? Ain't you heard? You can't cage no bird. Not for long," he said, and there was no smile in his voice, just

104

some kind of deadness. She felt sorry for him, somehow. It was as Lana said: "There's something about Sun Dog, isn't there? Makes you want to mother him?"

She turned her head a little to look at him through an opening in the brush. Even though he was wearing the same cutoffs he always wore, the ones with the pockets showing, he seemed different. He walked along beside her, appearing and disappearing from view. In another opening between shrubs she glimpsed bare brown arms and his bare upper body showing from under his old Harvard T-shirt. He had cut away the sleeves and cut a jagged circle out of the body so the word *Veritas* was taken away.

"How'd you get out? How'd you get out here?" she said, rubbing her neck.

"I couldn't miss the haying, now could I? That's what the sheriff told me, he told me about the hay. Isn't that right?"

"Have you seen Ty? Or anybody?" Lake said.

He didn't answer. She leaned into the scythe again, tried to get the rhythm back.

"Stop. Stop, just a minute, girl," he said. "I got something for you."

He pushed himself through the branches of an old forgotten rosebush left in the field. When he emerged there were tiny scratches oozing little domes of blood on his arms and shoulders.

"Here's the day's eye for you," he said, and offered Lake the field daisy he'd picked somewhere. She stared into the mustard yellow center and it did look like an eye. She wondered what the eye might be seeing. Something it had never seen before?

"That Ty, he's the eighth wonder of the world, ain't he?" Sun Dog said.

"What are you saying? I . . ." she began.

"Don't he never get weary? Don't he ever *stop*? You hear him out there? 'You want to eat this winter, work now!' He's got his motivating motor moving, that is sure."

"So?" Lake said. She was getting tired of standing out here in the hot sun, out here where there was no hiding place from herself or from everything that was going wrong with Barataria and her parents.

"So?" she said again. She threw her scythe onto the ground and the blade clanged against a rock. She moved into the shade offered by the hedgerow and sat down on the ground. She pulled petals from the daisy he'd given her and let them fall.

"Hey, what you doin'?" He put his hand over hers. "She loves me, she loves me not?"

He pulled the flower out of her hand and put the rest of it into his mouth. He watched her intently as he chewed and swallowed it. She didn't know what to say; she had to look away. It was as though he might swallow her up that way, make her disappear, take up her life for her. Finally he smiled that gap-toothed smile of his, and his eyes seemed to melt and shine and look into her full-faced and true as anything she had ever known. This time she didn't look away. Something like a laugh or a cry or both mixed up together bubbled inside her.

"It's awfully hot out here," was all she could say.

"I know just the cure for that, green-eyed lady."

He stood up and pulled her up beside him. His skin smelled warm, salty, and as familiar as her own. She felt hypnotized, almost in a trance. Opening a way through the brushy hedgerow, he led her along the edge of the oat field to the bank of the river. The closer they got, the faster they ran until, holding hands, they jumped into the brown river at its deepest place. At the depth of their plunge he swam up behind her and put his hands over her breasts and held her until they surfaced.

"Now, now, green-eyed girl, now," he said, and the river ran out of his mouth when he spoke.

They climbed up the riverbank and sat under a pine tree. She wanted to wrap her body around his more than anything in the world right now, and she let him kiss her again and again. Between kisses he sang to her under his breath those songs she had never heard before. But there was danger here. There were too many feelings crashing and churning around together inside her head. She felt as precarious as a cat lost in a tree not wanting to come down, afraid to go up. She pulled back, held her body away from his. When she could look at him, really look at him, she saw only the way he looked that day in town on his hands and knees in the dirt on the street. Where was the blue ageratum in his hair?

"I can't," was all she could say. "It's not . . . it's not right for me. Not now."

She let herself slip back into the river away from his gleaming eyes and his insistent hands and his songs, before she changed her mind. She floated away, letting the current move her downstream.

"You'll be back, I know you. I know you will," he yelled at her as she jackknifed deeper into the water.

Why can't you just go ahead and do it? Why not go all the way, the way Vernelle does? Kesey, too. You're actually the only one left in the whole world who hasn't made love to somebody. What was it Selene had said once? "Sometimes sex has something to do with love and sometimes it doesn't. Just make sure, whichever you choose, make sure you know the difference."

107

Watery scenes of life in the big, rambling family communes where she had always lived formed a wavery vision in
her mind. Pictures of the lovemaking she'd been a witness
to, pictures of love and sex and birth and death seemed to
float away together, rise up and disappear. Now, swimming
back upstream along the river bottom, Selene and Ty, Lana
and Andy, Halsey and Free, even Noble Justice and his
spaced-out women seemed to swim away together, holding
on to each other. With her arms spread like wings she
pulled herself to the surface and turned over on her back to
rest, let the river take her again, breathed in and out
slowly.

Finally, she knew what she wanted. Somewhere, some-
time in her life she did want the strong feelings she felt for
Sun Dog right now, but this wasn't the time or the place
and Sun Dog wasn't the person. What had he said that day
in the grassy nest, the day of her birthday, about not wanting to be too close to anyone? There were so many people
she *had* to love because of blood and circumstances: her
parents, the Barataria people, Grandmother. But there was
only one person whose love she could choose for herself.
She would be the only one to have anything to say about
him. Floating, she watched Sun Dog, lying on his back, on
the riverbank with one foot resting on the other propped-
up knee, waiting for her.

"Hey, Sun Dog." She stood up in a shallow place close to
the riverbank. "Hey."

She knew he would not hear her above the roar of the
river; she had only whispered the words.

14

When Lake got back to the hay field, all the workers, Barataria members and weekenders alike, were crowded around two picnic tables set along the west edge of the field. She looked into the sky, searching for the sun's place. It must have been eleven o'clock already. Lana and Free and a couple of the high-school kids, who probably thought this was a grand adventure, made stacks of peanut butter sandwiches from loaves of bread Free had baked the day before. There were bowls of alfalfa sprouts and nuts and seeds. And trays of cookies, usually forbidden cookies. It was Ty who had broken down and bought bags of chocolate chip cookies at the Piggly Wiggly.

Andy walked toward her as he fished a peach half out of the mason jar he carried. Lake wanted to remind him that it had been Selene who canned that very peach he ate off his knife blade.

"Where the hell'd you go?" Andy said. "You know you left a whole row unturned?"

Now suddenly she became aware of her wet clothes and dripping hair. Everyone would know she'd been in the river.

"You've been in the river? Playing hooky?" Free said, and raised his eyebrows. "Now I ask you, folks. Lake. Is that fair? We're all dying here . . ."

Without answering, she took a peanut butter sandwich and opened it to add strawberry jam. She felt as if everyone could see Sun Dog's hands, still pressed against her body, holding her.

"Hey, guys, Lakey's already had her one and only swim for the day. Right?" Chad said.

Kesey raised his fist in agreement. "Right!" he said.

Everyone laughed and somebody brought her a towel and tried to wring the water out of her hair for her and someone else handed her a glass of lemonade mixed with Kool-Aid. She took a big bite of bread. As she ate she thought about Sun Dog. Was he still back there at the river; how long would he wait for her to come to him? Somehow she understood that he would not wait long and wouldn't even care very much.

After lunch everyone went back into the fields to finish turning the grass in the windrows. It must have been one hundred degrees out there now. Lake walked along with the others, picking up grass with one hand and tossing it over her opposite shoulder so that the inert grass would lie more lightly on the ground. The grass was fresh and sweet and fine as hair, and Lake knew how important it was to let it dry. The task was restful and almost easy after the mowing. Others followed with rakes, and she saw the panicked insects rise and leap away from their clutch.

"If this stuff gets damp," Ty said, "it'll be good for nothing but compost. We need it for the animals. For bread. Hey, Lake! Everybody! Get moving. We want only the labor of the committed!"

*   *   *

It was midafternoon now. The sky glowed red with sun, heat still shimmered off the tin-roofed house, and the field was dotted with bundles of raked grass. Instead of the sound of the wind, the cicadas' noisy thrumming filled the air. The dogs barked farther and farther away in the fading light, and Halsey took the children belonging to the weekenders down to the river to swim. Lake leaned on her rake as Ty came toward her. He carried a cup of water he'd taken from the springhouse, and she saw how his hands were etched with tiny scratches from the hay.

"You want to tell me anything about this morning?" he said. "Where'd you go, Lake?"

Lake took a long drink of water before she spoke.

"I was with . . . well, I wasn't exactly *with* Sun Dog. We were . . . in the river. I wanted . . ."

Tyler put up both hands, palms toward her.

"Sun Dog? Wait a second. You were out there with Sun Dog? The old trickster? Lake, come on. You can do better than that. Just tell me it's none of my business. But don't lie, okay? Lying isn't worthy of you. Not like you to . . ."

"I don't lie, Tyler Gillespie," she said, and started to walk away from him. She would never tell him now, never tell him anything again.

"Well, I'm not accusing you . . ."

"Sure sounds like it to me."

"No, Lake, it's just that . . . Well, sure, I guess you didn't know . . ." Tyler picked up a stone and threw it out of the mowed field into a ditch.

"Sun Dog . . . Well, we have to protect Barataria. He's voted out, Lake. We worked too hard all these years to get them to accept us in town . . . you know that."

111

She couldn't think of anything to say.

"Besides that," Ty went on, "he's doing dope a lot. He knows the rules. Anyhow, we voted him out and so, anyhow, Lakey, Sun Dog is long gone. Free put him on a bus out of here early this morning."

They came in from the hay field riding on the tractor and crowded into the back end of the pickup with the rakes and scythes. Andy and Tyler sat in the front seat with Kesey, who practiced driving every chance he got. Lake was the first one to notice the house.

"Hey!" she said. "Look. The kids' house. Our house is all weird."

Shadows under the trees were dark enough now to make the house appear menacing, maybe like a box dropped from above by an alien spacecraft.

"Something *is* wrong with the kids' house!" Lake rapped on the back window of the cab and pointed.

"What the hell. . . ?" someone said.

Something was different, all right. Black paint ran down the colorful shutters as if someone had taken a bucketful and thrown it indiscriminately at the house. The rainbow arc on the red front door was gone, daubed over. Even the smeared windows looked like great empty eyes staring out of blank sockets. A black river of paint led into the front door. Before Kesey brought the truck to a full stop, Lake jumped out and began running. Her beautiful house!

She heard Andy charge out of the truck with Tyler right behind. Nobody took time to open the tailgate so the rest of the family jumped over the side as if they were dropping into a lifeboat. The tractor lumbered into the yard as the weekenders headed toward their cars parked up on the road. Trailing one behind the next, Andy, Ty, Chad, and

Lana ran single file down the path. For a moment no one said anything. It was as though they had never seen their house before. Lake ran ahead of the others. Avoiding the shining path of tacky paint, Lake pushed the door open with her foot.

With a new slash of black paint already smearing his army green undershirt, Andy came up fast behind Ty. He kicked an empty paint can and it clattered down the hill to the riverbank. Lake peered through the door and what she saw made her sick to her stomach. *Who could have done this?* Lake remembered the look on Mr. Willet's face, how Mr. Fox had looked at the ageratum on his shoe, how Sheriff Bailey had grinned in that new way. Maybe, she thought, it was the people in the checkered feed truck the night of the painting party?

"Wait," Tyler said. "Wait a minute. I'd better go in there first." He picked up a heavy stick blown down from the ash trees overhead in the high wind.

"You think it's someone, the men from town?" she whispered.

"No, now let's not jump to any conclusions here," Andy said, and put his hand on Tyler's arm.

Ty dropped the stick. "Yeah," he said, and breathed in noisily. "Yeah. I'll go see," and he pushed the door open wider and went inside.

Forcing herself to breathe, Lake tried to stop the peculiar hammering beat in her heart, in her pulses. She looked for some place to sit down, but there wasn't anything not covered with wet paint. *Where was Sun Dog?* Free had put him on a bus going someplace, but he wasn't on it. She knew that with her whole body.

"It's okay." Ty poked his head out of the front door. "Come on. You'd all better come in and see this."

113

Being careful not to step in the still wet trail of black paint leading into the house, everyone crowded into the little front room. They were so quiet Lake could hear a faraway train chugging up the mountain. Selene's looms, which had been moved into the house from the barn weeks ago, were pushed into the center of the room and all the linen warp had been slashed. The threads hung stiffly down into the works of the loom. A crude sixties peace sign was dribbled across her partly finished weaving. Only a little dusky light seeped into the room through the painted-over windows. Lake lit a lamp and held it over her head so everyone could see how the children's sleeping bags had been ripped open. The stuffing lay in gray wads on the floor.

"You think someone is trying to tell us something?" Free said, his eyes big behind his glasses.

"What happened to the dogs? Why didn't they bark? Scare the guy away?" someone said.

Lake remembered how the dogs feared Sun Dog, quivered whenever he came around them. It was a crazy idea and she brushed her hands across her eyes, erasing the thought, but another surged into its place like an ocean wave. It was a picture of the time she found him out in the potato field, sitting on the long, angled handle of a shovel he had jammed into the earth to the hilt, deep enough into the ground to hold his weight. He perched there on the shovel like a sad Peter Pan, peering at his fingernails, a sly look of the fox on his face. He said only that one of the dogs had died that morning.

Now Tyler wasn't saying anything, only folded his arms across his chest. He kicked at a pile of books with the toe of his boot.

"How do you figure. . . ?" he said finally. "A thing like this . . ."

114

Lake put her arm around his waist and leaned her head against his shoulder.

"Who do you suppose?" she asked him, as if he could take away the picture, the thoughts about Sun Dog. "Who did it?"

No one answered. Halsey and Lana had come in and they stood near a window as Lana tried to wipe paint off the sill with her shirttail. Chad cried and cursed as he stooped to pick one of the books out of the mess. Someone kicked an empty paint can and it clattered across the floor.

"Poor Sun Dog," someone said. "Poor Sun Dog worked so hard on our house."

"It's a good thing he's gone. He'd hate this," Lana said.

But Lake kept thinking. She remembered the way he smelled of dope more and more lately, the way he worked his charm game over and over, the way he played his tapes, hiding in his headset, rocking to the beat of a music only he could hear, not making music himself.

Tyler stirred the mess on the floor with his foot as if he were looking for something. In the center of the floor he found the old tin box where they kept all their earnings: the wood lot money, the wages Halsey and Sun Dog earned in town, the dollar bills from selling eggs at the farmers' market. Someone had taken it from Lana's desk in the kitchen. No one ever locked anything there, Lake thought. It would have been easy. Now the box was open, empty. Ty said nothing. He looked old and tired to Lake; for the first time in her life she saw him the way he'd be in twenty years. First Selene and then school and the worry about the hay and now this. He sagged heavily into an overstuffed chair and put his head down onto one of the fat arms. They all stopped what they were doing, watched him, waited for some action, some statement. Lake idly wrote her name with a strand of Selene's yarn pressed into the still damp black paint.

"God! Oh, God! The son of a . . ." Tyler yelled. It was almost a scream. "Here it is. I should have seen it coming."

He jumped up from his chair, handed a piece of paper to Free.

"Sun Dog?" Free said. "You're kidding? Sun Dog!"

Everyone gathered around Ty then, with their hands covering their mouths, a terrible truth showing on their faces, while Free read the note from Sun Dog to them.

> i'm off to see the wizard, people, the wonderful
>   wizard
> of wires, it is. and i'm not going to let them catch
>   me now.
> do they say me and you never have known
> what happens next?
> nothing's linear, here. like your latest design for
>   living. Ty
> Lake,
> careful what you need, you might want it. plus
>   words to that effect.
> empty empty empty here and there and
>   everywhere. i go some place
> warm to sing my songs.   again

Except for taking care of the chickens and the cow, nothing more was done on the farm in what was left of the day. No one had the heart to fix any supper, and they left the litter of the Children's House as they had found it. The children could sleep in the barn or in the Big House, they said. They could only stare through the paint-blackened windows as if they might see something to make them understand. Finally, because there was nothing left to do,

116

they wandered one by one down to the small barn or the Big House, where they discovered that Sun Dog had visited them there, too. Dresser drawers and sleeping bags, even the space between mattress and bed springs, had been searched. Money, maybe their little hidden cache of contraband drugs, their jewelry, were gone.

Lake climbed the steps to the loft. She wanted, finally, to see if he had touched (the way he touched her?) the river stones she saved, the poems she wrote, Selene's ring, the music box Grandmother sent long ago, the old cigar box filled with bits of her life. But he had left no mark upstairs. There was no paint dribbled across the floor of her tiny space; the windows were untouched. She lay down on her sleeping bag and buried her nose in it. Maybe there was another odor there, not just her own. There was nothing.

She closed her eyes, remembering the river and how Sun Dog's lips, cushioned in his fine, fringy beard and mustache, felt on hers. And then she let her mind wander back to the day when the sheriff came to tell them Sun Dog was in the jail. Now she understood why she had hidden the necklace of strange coins he gave her in the bottom of her sleeping bag. She hadn't worn it again. Frantically she shook out her bed roll, waiting for the *rustle-clink* of the necklace as it hit the floor. There was no sound. Of course. She was no different from the others after all. Smiling his gap-toothed smile, he had ignored her sign THIS SPACE RESERVED FOR LAKE.

Later, led by physical hunger, they all gathered, unspeaking, in the kitchen, where they went about fixing a cold supper. Moving from refrigerator to sink to bread box, fixing just enough for themselves, they tried to stay out of each other's way. Lake couldn't eat. She knew that they had behaved as if there were no ownership and no privacy,

117

and Sun Dog knew that. She pictured him fingering through everyone's things, invading their small privacies even though they themselves hadn't valued privacy as much as they valued trust. He had stolen the flotsam and jetsam of their lives and loves, taken tangible, solid things from them; but the theft of privacy was much worse, she thought. How could he betray the family when they were all so open to him, to everybody, to the whole world?

Still, the anger gradually wore off. Lake thought they used it up talking, talking. She almost had to laugh at the way it turned out. First the talking was done in groups of two or three, then in bigger clusters of people shaking fists and kicking stones in the barnyard. Then the words all rumbled up like the ocean and a wave of them crashed, breaking into a special meeting. No one knew who called the meeting—it just seemed to happen.

Before she came into the community room Lake put a blue mason jar filled with flowers in the center of the room. They weren't Sun Dog's usual bouquet of hothouse carnations stolen from Rafferty's Florist in town, but blue chicory and fringey wild asters and yellow-eyed daisies. Someone brought lighted candles. It was as if someone had died and this was the funeral.

"There's going to be a long time of mourning," Lana began. "We've had, you know, a loss, big loss."

Andy said they needed to exorcise Sun Dog's bad vibes out of their midst so they could get right again.

"Yeah . . . we have to work through it," Free said.

Ty said, "Right. But we're not going to let the action of one person dictate our behavior. We have to keep our own way of being in the world."

Lake sat on the floor between Lana and Andy. Andy's bulky warmth and Lana's sinewy arm around her waist seemed to personify the strength of the family. As they locked arms in the good, familiar circle, facing one another so that they saw one another's tears, they told stories about Sun Dog, the good and evil of him. When it came Lake's turn to speak she said, "I guess I love him and I guess I hate him, too. And that's the hardest part of all." Tears ran down her cheeks, and she wiped them away with her hand. Lana squeezed her hand and kissed her. "Maybe he was your first love. You never forget your first love, especially when it turns out like this," she whispered.

As the talk flowed around the circle and the candles flickered out, the only picture Lake could bring to mind was of Sun Dog lying on the bank of the river with one foot on the other propped-up knee, waiting. She didn't understand why she had left him there. Maybe, she wondered, it had something to do with all the lessons she'd learned here at Barataria, lessons about thinking long-term, about patience, about doing what was needed in each season of your life. She closed her eyes. Someone was singing now. Sun Dog's song about having no home. Now her vision changed. She saw Sun Dog's face, with his silky beard and his melting brown eyes, take the place reserved for the brooding James Dean posters in Vernelle's room.

15

There had been a week or two of good weather. Ty listened to the hog and corn futures on the radio every day, alfalfa and clover were seeded over the oats, a small fire in the washhouse was put out before it damaged anything, and a notice of registration and orientation at the consolidated high school came at last. A bus routing map was enclosed. Ty ripped up the forms and the thick cardboard schedule and threw them into the wood stove. Lake decided it was time to take things into her own hands.

She found her father in the barn, up in the loft stacking bales of straw. Beads of sweat bloomed on his upper lip and he wore jeans held up with a piece of rope around his thin—too thin—waist. He looked the way he had during the drought last year, when everything smelled of dust and the corn folded in on itself.

"You think you could cut loose of your time for a minute and listen to me? Just a minute? There's something that has to be done," Lake said.

Without speaking Ty sat down on a bale of blue-green alfalfa and looked down at her.

120

"I wrote to Grandmother," she said. "I want to go up there and go to school. I thought we should talk about it."

"God, Lake," Tyler said. "Aren't you pretty intense all of a sudden? Let's not do anything to end our choices, now."

"No, not really. But I've been thinking, Ty, I'm getting too old for you to teach me now. You know, chemistry and Spanish three and all that? You'd have to be state certified or something. Besides, you don't have time with all the farm work." She didn't say that two of the best workers, Selene and Sun Dog, were gone now, but that was true, too. And there was no telling what Sun Dog's actions had done to their chances of ever getting another job in town. Leaning against a post, she fingered the adz mark in the hand-hewn oak. When she got a splinter in her hand, she sucked at it, looking at Ty, trying to be straight and open the way he'd want her to be.

"I'll be a senior in September," she said. "And I want to think about that, make plans."

Tyler climbed down and stood on the plank floor, ankle-deep in straw, looking at his boots as if he'd never seen boots before.

"It's okay," he began. "You don't have to go through all that. Just do what they say. Go on. Go over to the consolidated school . . . we'll work it out," he said. "I mean . . . some way or another we'll get right here."

"No, I've thought about that, too," Lake said. "It's no good. I'm not going to ride the bus three hours a day. I'd hate it. You'd hate it. It's anti everything you believe. You know: wasted gas, wasted hours sitting staring out the window? I couldn't even do homework on the bus. I'd throw up. And there wouldn't be any time left over to work around here with you."

Ty paced back and forth, kicking up little piles of yellow straw as he walked. Lake wanted to tell him the other reason—the real reason—she had to leave, but she wasn't sure she could explain it, wasn't sure he'd understand. She didn't understand it herself, but it had something to do with Selene, maybe everything to do with Selene's leaving. Lake wanted to know more about her blood family, about her grandmother. In a way it was as if she were adopted and knew only fragments about where she really came from.

If she went up to Michigan, maybe she could understand more about why Selene had run away in the first place and why she had to abandon the Barataria dream. Dreams change, she knew, and now it was time to find out how and why.

She asked herself what she could do to help Ty now. It looked as if the farm were doomed; there was no way they could make it work. Too much had happened, too much bad weather, too many workers deserting the farm, too little money to tide them over. Why should she stay there and watch it all go down? She couldn't stand that. If Selene had to start over to grow a new life, why wasn't it right for her to try it, too?

"Ty, listen," she said.

Lake moved closer to her father, as if she could touch him and that would help her understand.

"Did you really write to your grandmother?"

"Yes."

"You hear back?"

"No, there hasn't been time. But I'm going anyhow. She took us in once before . . . she'll have to . . ."

"She doesn't have to, Lake. That was eight, nine years ago. She's got a life."

"Yes, she will. She'll want me, I know it."

Later Lake hitched a ride to town in the pickup with Lana and Andy. When they ran out of gas Lake walked the rest of the way, but Lana and Andy went back to the farm, too discouraged to try to find gas and not motivated enough to walk further. Lake was glad for the walk and the time alone. It gave her time to plan out what she would say to Vernelle, how she could borrow bus fare from her for the ride to Michigan. Although Vernelle was generous, asking her would be hard, Lake decided. After all, Vernelle was the one who had tried to be friends again. It was Lake who had avoided her, half embarrassed and half angry that Vernelle had been the one to tell her she wasn't welcome in Shellerton Forge School. Now, as she walked along the highway, Lake convinced herself that she'd actually be doing Vernelle a favor. If she lent Lake the money, Vernelle would be totally in character, eager to be magnanimous, be friends again.

Lake was hot and sweaty when she sat down on the revolving stool at the marble counter. Before Vernelle had even opened up the pot of hot fudge or spooned whipped cream over the sundae she made for Lake (as if nothing unusual had happened), Lake asked her for the $32.50. Vernelle said sure, why not? Between bites of the sundae, Lake explained that she didn't know how or when she could repay Vernelle. And Vernelle told Lake she had enough to worry about.

"I hate to see you go, but you'll be back," Vernelle said. "I know you. You'll be back here sure as God made little green apples."

It was a long night and an even longer day on the big Greyhound, and when Lake arrived in Bay View she real-

123

ized she remembered nothing at all about where her grandmother's house might be.

"Sure, you can walk it. You don't need a taxi," the man in the ticket cage said. "It's only a half mile, maybe a mile. Just take Ferry Street out to the Bay Road. Andover is three, maybe four blocks east off Bay."

As she walked along she remembered the green aisle formed by maples reaching for each other overhead. Nothing else seemed familiar. She knew the address by heart, though, and repeated it to herself as she read the brass numbers on white fences or on mailboxes designed to look like ducks. *Five-seventy. Six hundred. Six-ten. Six-twenty-six. There it was.*

The latticed entranceway, the green shutters, and tiled roof brought back more memories as she walked up the gravel driveway. She pictured the way the rooms were laid out inside, but there was only a sense of dim coolness, of quiet, and of large windows letting in light from the top of a stairway. She had watched "Father Knows Best" somewhere inside until Tyler pulled out the plug. That was only the first of the differences between Ty and Selene and her grandmother that Lake had noticed that spring.

No one answered her first ring. Nor the second. She heard the two-note bell sound inside, gentle, distant, and musical, as if a bell had been tolled in a cave. Then there was silence. A car drove by slowly. The driver, a man wearing a wide-brimmed hat, peered out at her over the steering wheel. In her faded jeans, loose shirt, and worn sandals, and with her long hair and dirty duffel, she knew she looked like some sort of alien creature invading this perfect street.

Staring out at the busy road, she put her hands in her pockets. Maybe she hadn't done the right thing after all.

Why had she come to live with a grandmother she barely remembered, someone who had sent her mother away so long ago? She ought to be back on the farm where everything was familiar. The words *familiar* and *family* were so alike, she thought. She rubbed her face with both hands and closed her eyes. A picture flashed into her mind's eye. It was a time soon after her seventh birthday.

Tyler and Selene put their fingers to their lips, wrap her in blankets, and carry her downstairs. Noble Justice is asleep across the hall with his door open. Ty's beard scratches against Lake's face. They take nothing with them, the truck Ty paid for, their clothes, none of Selene's weaving and pottery. Nothing, Ty says. Let's just get out of this place. He says Noble Justice's rules are as false as his made-up name. Lake doesn't understand why they are leaving now, why they didn't leave long ago, when Noble Justice claimed her while Tyler just stood there and Selene disappeared. She cannot forget it even as her father carries her, weeping with joy and relief.

They should not be on the road. Even Lake knows this. The VW doesn't start half the time. All the way from Colorado they sleep in the van and use quarters from Selene's old blue mason jar for gas. They eat little because they are sick with some kind of dysentery and fever, which had spread through the house. They use rest stop bathrooms or pull off the road and squat in the long grass, even Ty. Selene hides Lake behind her long skirts. When they run out of quarters, Selene moves gracefully between cars lined up at gas pumps with a handmade basket in hand. She smiles and bows for the people while Lake can only curl herself under blankets in the back seat, sweating and crying. She thinks that Selene will begin to sing and dance next. Ty keeps his head down. His eyes are blank and he tinkers with the smeary blue van.

Selene dumps coins into Ty's greasy hands and laughs, and says, So what, it isn't the first time and maybe not the last, right?

Ty laughs and they hug each other and stop to smoke a joint of marijuana. This is the last of it, they say as they roll the weed into a thin paper.

In Ohio the tires begin to go. With each flat tire Ty's patience leaks out through his dirty fingernails and Lake feels the vibrations of his anger as he bends to undo the lug nuts one more time. After the fourth flat the spare can't be patched one more time.

We're heading for your mother's, Ty says. We're closer to your mother's than any place I can think of.

Selene says, No. I'm not going back there with my tail between my legs. She'll never—

We have to. We've got to regroup. No choices left here. We wait there for the trust money.

Selene doesn't argue anymore. Lake stares out the window at telephone poles whizzing by. Rainwater needles in at her, but she doesn't say anything. Carbon monoxide poisoning. Their muffler is strewn in pieces all the way back to Colorado. They see the big lake, Lake St. Clair. It borders the suburb near Detroit where Grandmother Thurston lives. Lake sees how the trees touch each other above them, making a leafy aisle.

And then in the center of Andover Street, the VW dies. Ty sits there, shakes his head back and forth as if there are windshield wipers, which there are not. He says nothing. It is a dangerous sign, Lake thinks. He gets out of the van slowly, opens the rear door, and reaches inside. Lake doesn't know what her predictable father will do with the *sledgehammer he takes in both hands. Rain runs off the brim of his wide hat. He raises the hammer and it thuds into the door he has closed leaving Lake and Selene inside. Ty gets the driver's side door, the grille, even the wheels. The VW rocks back and forth and there is the sound of metal falling. Selene covers her face with her hands, shakes her head. Lake rocks in rhythm with the shaking van, watches her father with a strange light in her eyes, as if she is learning something permanent here.*

Perhaps, she thinks, Grandmother will come out of the big gray house and stop the next thing from happening. But she doesn't come. Selene gets out of the van, pulls Lake out, and they walk slowly up the driveway in the rain. They stand on the front porch under a curved archway and water runs down Selene's face and drips onto her shirt. She rings the bell and waits. Lake wonders why her mother doesn't walk right in the front door the way people do when they come home.

Lake rang the bell again. When no one answered she picked up her duffel and started down the steps. There was a flash of red across the yard and around the side of the gray-shingled house. She waited. Could it have been Grandmother? Nothing moved. Only a cardinal sang somewhere out of sight. She put the duffel down on a white slatted bench built into the arched lattice. There was another bench across from it. She sat down and stared at pink geraniums in a ceramic pot. Selene would hate them, she thought. Selene hated pink. There were pink and yellow flowers mixed with pale green plants lining the driveway, in beds beneath tall windows, as if someone had planned a specific color scheme. Selene would hate it, all right. Hadn't she hated it enough to leave it?

But Selene wasn't there. No one knew where she was for sure. Only some message about singing background on commercials in Nashville. Ty wasn't there, either. She knew, though, exactly where Ty would be. He would be chopping wood, hot-wiring one of the tractors, or standing up at meeting, talking talking talking about his dream of a new, sustainable world. She was on her own, she knew. She was the one who had chosen to come here to find her grandmother. She was the one who was tired and hungry.

There must be someone around. Crossing the driveway, she followed a grassy path to a large square garden fenced in with chicken wire. Laid out exactly like Selene's garden with tall staked tomatoes in back and rows of green beans on string fences, it was edged with orange and red marigolds, also just like Selene's. There was a large fenced-in swimming pool in the background. Grandmother knelt there with a trowel in her hand and a large basket beside her. Lake tried to speak, but no sound came when she opened her mouth. She swallowed hard and tried again. It was her grandmother who spoke first.

"Lake? Oh. It's Lake!" She shaded her eyes with her hands. Her voice made a shiver of some new kind of pleasure run up Lake's spine.

Grandmother didn't get up, but knelt there looking into the earth.

"Look at this, will you?" she said.

Lake came closer and knelt down beside her grandmother, who seemed smaller than she remembered, her hair like a dandelion gone to seed. A sudden wind showered them with feathery seeds and locust blossoms that had hung on the tree too long.

"Anemones," her grandmother said. "The anemones are

128

blooming again. They were bounteous this spring and now look, they are doing it again."

The flowers were low to the ground, pink, yellow, or red, with purple throats or deep blue cuplike blossoms. Lush-looking next to the vegetables and the plain grass, the flowers were beautiful, unexpected.

"They're nice."

Lake found her voice, but couldn't imagine why her grandmother acted as if she'd been gone only for an hour or so instead of nine years. Grandmother picked one of the flowers and offered it to Lake.

"Wind flowers," she said. "And just look what the wind blew in."

16

Carrying a woven basket hooked over her arm, Grandmother led Lake onto the glassed-in back porch. In one corner there was a tree in a pot growing up through a hole in the roof. She had never seen a living tree right inside the house before, and she wondered if Selene knew it was there. It seemed like something Selene would do. Grandmother stopped at French doors opening into the living room to slip off her shoes. Lake did the same, feeling the carpet soft and spongy beneath her bare feet. When Lake saw the stone fireplace and the chimney corner filled with embroidered pillows, a window on one side of it, the chimney breast on the other, she was overcome with a feeling of familiarity.

Surely the old destroyed VW was still parked out in front; Tyler and Selene would be in the hall, dripping rain onto the shining brick floors. Lake remembered how she had pushed past them that day, heading for the nest of colored pillows in the chimney corner, as if she were a salmon swimming upstream. She hadn't moved from that safe haven for two days except to eat, and Grandmother let her sleep there the whole time, holding Selene's Raggedy Ann.

Lake would have stopped there now to curl up in the pillows, but Grandmother hurried on through the dining room and into the kitchen.

"Sit there, will you, and talk to me, Lake, while I finish getting dinner ready? I'm starved. When did you eat last? I know you're starving, too," she said.

The large kitchen where Grandmother set the basket of tomatoes and salad greens on the counter was filled with appliances, what Ty would have called "better living through electricity." The windows were almost covered with pale tendrils of ivy reaching across the windowsill, searching for a way inside. The light filtering through the leaves cast a golden green glow across the whole room. While Lake waited at a small wrought-iron table, Grandmother put her lettuces into a colander and washed them, poured boiling water over the largest of the tomatoes, big and red as seed catalog pictures, and pulled the skin off. Selene skinned tomatoes that way. It was strange the way so much here reminded Lake of her mother. She hadn't thought about her mother this much in weeks. Somehow being here in Grandmother's house, away from Barataria and Ty's strong influence, she felt her mother's presence. Grandmother hadn't asked about Selene yet. Lake wondered what she would call her, Selene or Eliza.

Lake was unable to move to help her grandmother. She was overwhelmed by the differences between Grandmother's house and Barataria. The buzzing of the microwave, the spices on a shelf in alphabetical order . . .

"Let's go," Grandmother said, carrying their filled plates into the dining room.

Lake followed with the tomatoes on an oval cut-glass dish. Taking up the heavy white napkin from the polished table, Grandmother gave it a flick of her wrist so that it fell

131

open with a soft, thick, muffled sound. Conscious of the weight of the napkin across her blue-jeaned knees, its whiteness contrasted with her dirty fingernails, Lake did the same. A cut-glass bowl filled with yellow roses reflected blue light from the candles onto the table. There were more roses in the wallpaper and someone had painted cabbage roses on the china plates; pale pink and green, drooping and heavy like the real ones in the bowl. Lake ran her finger around the gold-edged rim of her plate and inhaled slowly. The sweet-scented roses had covered over the smell of their dinner. It wasn't like the farm where what you smelled was definitely the cabbages, not the roses.

"These are Better Boys," Grandmother said as she handed the plate of tomato slices to Lake. "I tried them this year for a change. And what a bounteous gift they gave me. You look famished. Eat now, Lake. I hope you like the parsley sprinkled on top."

Following her grandmother's example, Lake chose the large silver fork at the side of her plate. Its design was as ornate and complicated as Sun Dog's belt buckle and she stared at it, heavy in her hand. Lake felt as though she'd been living on another planet, maybe, as though she'd never known certain ways of living. For a moment she couldn't raise the fork to her mouth. She couldn't seem to think of anything to say. Grandmother hadn't asked her how she had gotten there.

She opened her mouth and the only words to come out were "We save . . . we save our own seeds. Every year."

Oh no, why did I say that? she asked herself.

"What a nice way to do it. If you have the time," Grandmother said. "I have to run over to the K mart to buy mine. Burpee? In a package?"

Dishes, candles, silver, everything on the table sparkled

132

and shone; even the food itself was pleasant to look at. Things are going to be different here, Lake thought. Only one person at a time in the kitchen. No steamed-up windows to write on, no good-natured jostling and singing, everyone working together. No dipping bread or fingers in the stew, no smell of baking bread, no great kettles of rice and soup beans, and no mugs of cider heated to hide the fact that it had turned.

This was only her first meal with Grandmother, but she already saw, as if through her grandmother's eyes, the way the farm children grabbed bread or stole gingersnaps off the bare table to hide for later. At Barataria people spent a lot of time foraging for extra food because the amount of food and its taste was dependent on the garden produce or on whose turn it was to cook. No one was ever late for meals no matter what was served, and Lake knew it was the same here with her grandmother, but for different reasons.

Drinking in the quiet, the lush richness of linen and golden candlelight, she sighed and put her hands in her lap. The still air surrounding Grandmother seemed to embrace Lake while it cast a shadow over the tumult of everything she had grown up with. As she gazed at her reflection in the mirrored wall across from her place at the shining table, she couldn't even feel disloyal.

Lake ate the tomatoes and the cold, sliced turkey breast and the tiny zucchini in a creamy sauce.

"That's the Alfredo sauce you get ready-made at Bay Road Market. I buy the sauce, freeze it, and then pop it in the microwave." Grandmother waved her hand at the ease of it.

Lake had eaten nothing since she had waved good-bye to Tyler and all the others the night before, but somehow she was too tired to eat. She was road weary, Tyler would have said, more tired than she had ever been, even after haying time. When Grandmother went into the kitchen with their plates, she leaned her head against the tall-backed chair. She knew she had eaten too little and too fast and hadn't talked enough or said anything real and had sometimes stared at her plate with her elbows on the table. Grandmother didn't ask questions about anything. In her deep breathy voice, without waiting for Lake to join in, she talked about her garden, the anemones, the daylilies, the drought, and how a group she belonged to had finally gotten the city interested in a wetlands ordinance.

Lake wasn't used to this impersonal talk with nothing about sorting out feelings or experiences, no real connection. Was it because Grandmother was too polite to ask personal questions? Was that it? She wanted to say something about why she had come, to face all those questions and be straight and clear the way Ty and Selene had taught her, but she was too tired to think. Besides, she wasn't sure anymore why she had come and what she would do now that she was here. If she hadn't fit into Shellerton Forge, how would she possibly fit in here?

Lake pulled herself up straighter in the soft chair. In the quiet she heard the faint clink of ice cubes melting against each other in her glass. There was the tranquil, muffled ticktock of a clock somewhere deep in the house, and from the kitchen Grandmother's voice seemed to buzz and fade out like a radio-station signal on a long trip. Something about peach pie. Fresh Michigan peaches, she heard. Lake folded her hands in her lap and sighed again. And then suddenly she felt herself being helped up from her chair and led up the stairs. Grandmother's thin muscular arm was around her waist, supporting her. She heard the clock on the landing closer now, or was it her grandmother's heartbeat she heard?

"Child, child. You are simply worn out," Grandmother was saying as she opened a white paneled door at the top of the stairs.

"I'm giving you Eliza's . . . your mother's room," she said. "You may remember it from last time?"

Lake remembered the bank of six tall windows facing the gardens in back and how bright it had been during the naps that Grandmother had insisted she take each afternoon.

"You may decide later if you like it . . . Come in," Grandmother said.

The windows were still there, covered by white ruffled curtains that stirred as they came into the room. The cool night air wakened Lake a little. Everything was blue—blue walls, blue carpeting, a blue chintz-covered settee and chairs—all the color of the sky. Lake was more awake now, taking it all in. There was a tall dresser and two beds; one a double bed and the other a narrow bed on tall thin legs. She remembered the little stool she used to climb aboard as if it were a ship. Lake pictured her mother in this room the way she was before Lake was born, sitting by the windows reading about Holden Caulfield and Robert Kennedy and Martin Luther King, doodling peace signs on the pages or listening to Joan Baez and Bob Dylan and the Beatles.

"See. Here it is," her grandmother said. "I can't tell you it looks the same as it did when your mother lived here. I think it's been done over twice since those days."

Was there a shadow on Grandmother's deeply lined face, or was it simply that it was getting dark and the sun had set behind the sloping garden? Grandmother opened a closet door.

"Your mother's things are still in there," she said. "Scrapbooks, yearbooks. Look here—those old prom dresses. I'd almost forgotten how she . . ."

Books lined the top shelves and there were three or four strapless dresses, pink and white satin, hanging on padded pink hangers. A row of plastic shoe boxes filled with colored shoes stood on the floor.

"Let's talk about tomorrow, Lake." Grandmother looked at her directly.

Lake thought of Sun Dog for some reason and the way he looked straight at you, stared at you from a long way away trying, he said, to make a connection with you. This was better than the surface talk at dinner.

Now, although they looked nothing alike, Grandmother seemed more like Selene. Selene was small and almost feathery. Grandmother was thin, too, but she was all angles and purpose and energy with that shock of wispy white hair cropped short as a boy's.

"Sure," Lake said. "That's no problem, what?"

"You're already a week or so late for registration and so we have to get you to school next Monday so you can get the courses you want. And, Lake, if you are going to stay with me, and I think you are, we'll have to have a few rules, hours and boys and, you know, things. I mean, I'm gone a lot. It's the house we're restoring—the Historical Society—and I don't want to have to worry. I'm sure you understand. I haven't had any *teenagers* in the house for so long a time and . . ."

Lake wasn't sure she liked having Grandmother tell her she had to go to school, even though that is what she planned to do. Ty and Selene never *told* her she had to attend school; she had always chosen school over anything else. And she couldn't think what all the rules about boys and hours might be.

136

"I . . . we don't usually have regulations," Lake said, remembering how Vernelle had envied the Barataria kids and the way they lived without curfew, without even driver's licenses.

"I mean, I just thought . . ." Lake wasn't used to explaining herself to an adult and something about the look on her grandmother's face, the lengthening of her neck and back, stopped her before she said more.

"We'll just go over to school, Lake, after you're rested and we'll see if they can keep you in your grade. That rural school . . ." Grandmother's voice trailed off. She said nothing more about the rules.

"I have a question, too, for you," Lake went on as her grandmother turned back the white coverlet on the tall bed.

"Certainly, Lake. That's the best way. That way we'll get along. Be friends. Okay?"

"Well." Lake pushed back the curtain and looked out over the gardens. There were little lights everywhere and car lights moving back and forth in the distance. "I don't know . . ."

"Don't know what?" Grandmother flicked on a bed lamp that shown yellow over the pillow.

". . . Don't know what I should call you." Selene had never had a real name for her mother and had referred to her only as "your grandmother."

"Well, why not call me Grand? Everyone else does. It's the name I was born with, Jeannette Grand Flemming. Thurston when I married your grandfather. Grand is a family name. One of your maternal great-greats."

"Okay," Lake said. "Grand it is."

The name seemed to fit and it was as if Lake had known it all along. She picked up her duffel and put it on the

137

settee and then unzipped her jeans and let them fall to the floor.

"Oh," Grand said, staring at Lake's bare brown legs. "Well. I'll just let you get to bed. The shower is there."

She left the room quickly, closing the door behind her. Lake marveled at the way the door fit into its frame and closed perfectly and completely. Somehow it was satisfying to hear that click, and she thought about her space in the upper loft of the Children's House where she didn't even have a curtain to protect her privacy. She slipped off her sandals and her feet looked gray and dirty against the pale carpeting. Maybe she didn't fit here in this perfect room, in this perfect house, with this perfect grandmother. But there was something deep inside that told her she did belong. There was a flush of excitement and she felt wide awake now.

She would take that shower Grand mentioned. As Lake slipped her shirt off over her head, there was a soft knock on the door.

"Are you decent?" Grandmother whispered.

"Decent?" Lake laughed out loud. "Oh, sure. Decent? Yeah."

The door opened and then closed again fast when Grand saw Lake standing there wearing nothing except her underpants. Her grandmother spoke through the closed door.

"Oh, I *am* sorry. I don't usually barge in on people like that. I thought you . . . When you are . . ." Grand flustered.

"Honest, I'm okay. Fine." Lake opened the door.

Grandmother shut it. "No. Well, when you put something on I . . ."

Lake hurried to open her duffel and put on a T-shirt.

"There. Is that better?" she said as she opened the door. "I guess I'm not used to doors and, well, you know."

"No, I guess not," Grandmother said. "And it has been a long time since I've had any young people . . ."

Lake put her hand on her grandmother's shoulder.

"We're going to make it okay. Honest, we are," she said. She wanted to hug her grandmother, hold her the way her parents and everyone else on the farm did every day and every night, but Grand moved away.

"Oh, before I forget, one more thing." Grand pointed to the closet. "Just hang your things in there. I think there are enough hangers and everything for you. Just shove those old things of your mother's back."

"Thanks," Lake said, knowing that she didn't have anything to put there except one of Selene's tie-dyed skirts and a few T-shirts.

In the bathroom, when she saw how complicated all the handles and nozzles were, she decided against a shower. She turned out the lights, and using the little footstool to climb into bed she fell back against the pillows. Traffic sounds came through the open window, and if she tried hard enough, she could make them sound like the river down the hill from the Children's House. She closed her eyes, but as tired as she was she could not sleep in this tall narrow bed on thin legs. Unrolling her sleeping bag, she lay down on the floor and went to sleep dreaming about the chimney corner and Selene's Raggedy Ann doll.

17

Monday morning Grand took Lake to school.

"Don't you think you've soaked up enough TV to make up for lost time?" she said. "Come on. Let's find out the next chapter of your life."

It was true what Grand said about television. All weekend before breakfast, long after dinner, and after Grand had gone up to bed, Lake lay on the sofa in Grand's darkened family room letting the sound and action on the screen flow around her, hypnotize her. All those images in full color and living sound, as Grand described it, left her feeling ashamed that she had no taste, no discretion. She knew what Ty and the others would say if they could see her. They'd say she was becoming one of those open-mouthed, slump-shouldered people, lying on overstuffed couches, pushing buttons, eating white bread and nitrite-filled bologna sandwiches.

Still, even with all her self-criticism, she watched everything as if TV were a lifeline to something she had almost missed. It all seemed so important, so real and so much easier than anything else.

"Eliza used to watch a lot of TV. Must come with the

age. Sixteen," Grand said with a funny little smile hovering around her eyes. "Funny, I never said 'Haven't you got anything better to do?' to her."

Sometimes Lake fell asleep on the sofa in front of the flickering blue screen and dreamed the same dream she'd dreamed for a long, long time: the one about struggling to catch a train only to find that she had no ticket and had to watch the train disappear down the tracks without her.

Seated now in the administration offices at Bay View East High School, Lake waited for the principal to appear. She had written pages of exams for grade placement, and while she worked Grand filled out all the proper guardianship forms, enrolling her.

"Well, you're all set. It's official." She poked her head in the door of the principal's office. "I'll have to be leaving now. I have a meeting," Grand added. "I'll pick you up at three o'clock. You could walk home if I'm not. . . ? No, no, never mind. Just wait out there by the kiosk in the parking lot. Make it ten after. Three-ten. I'm sure I'll be finished by three-ten. Okay?"

Her grandmother hurried down the long, shining, empty hallway, leaving Lake alone to wait for Philip Westcote, the principal. He arrived, a youngish man wearing thick-lensed, rimless glasses that made him look so much like Free that Lake felt a sudden wave of homesickness. Surely she wouldn't cry now. She looked down at her lap.

"Well, who have we here? Miss . . . uh?" The principal looked down at the papers on his desk.

"I'm Lake," she said. "Gillespie. Lake Gillespie."

He looked up, eyes wide. "Lake? Lake," he said as if he had to think about it. "Yes, Miss Gillespie."

She didn't recognize herself as a "Miss Gillespie" in this

141

gigantic school set on acres of land as if it were a university. This school had a parking lot for students' cars and a patio where they smoked and drank Coke, tennis courts and baseball diamonds, two of them. Suddenly she missed Kesey and Chad . . . Vernelle, too. She'd have to write Vernelle a letter and tell her thanks for the money. Then she'd add a postscript about how she understood now that Vernelle was only trying to help when she told her about what the school board was doing. It hadn't been her fault then and it wasn't now. Lake longed for the old red brick, two-story building at Shellerton Forge with its wooden floors and high ceilings, even if her friends did have to sneak smokes behind the furnace or in the girls' bathroom.

"You've done very well, Miss Gillespie." Mr. Westcote flipped the pages of her test booklet. "Where did you say you'd been in school?"

"Shellerton Forge. That's in central Kentucky," she said. And then, "But until my freshman year, it was mostly my parents and . . . people, our family, friends we lived with? They taught us at home. Home school?"

Why was she suddenly apologetic about being taught at home? She had done well, hadn't he said she'd done well?

"Well, Miss Gillespie—Lake, is it? Your test scores are quite impressive." He ran his finger down a column of figures. "Oh," he paused, "what about a language? We have a language requirement for graduation."

"I had a little Spanish," she said. "One of our members, someone who lived with . . ."

She didn't know how to describe Barataria and all its variety to Mr. Westcote, but she rushed on about José Carlos, the fisherman from California who had lived on the farm a few years ago, and how he talked to her in Spanish and how they translated his stories and songs into English together.

"Fine. Yes," he kept reading. "You will need more science, too, but it appears you've fulfilled our writing requirement, our history . . . Very nice. Talk to your adviser about honors classes. I think you qualify, but of course that would be her department."

Mr. Westcote leaned back in his leather-covered swivel chair.

"Whoever was in charge of your secondary education seems to have done a good job," he said. "Do you like school, Miss Gillespie?"

He didn't wait for her answer, began gathering up her test booklets and papers.

"We'll get you into the computer now. In that department. Out there."

From the big sunny room, filled with students and secretaries, came the muffled sound of voices, typewriters, and telephones. She'd never seen so many different kinds of people—African-American kids, Japanese, East Indians, teachers, young and old. Some wore sunglasses on top of their heads like another pair of eyes, and others wore them to cover their eyes, even inside the school.

"Just go down the main hall to Ms. Appleton's. She's our senior adviser," Mr. Westcote continued. "Well. Well, then. Tomorrow, well, it looks as if you'll be a full-fledged senior." He rubbed his hands together. "You might even test out . . . Well, Ms. Appleton will work all that out for you. That'll be her department. She's in the library, down the main hall."

Standing, he handed her a sheaf of papers and stuck out the other hand. They shook hands.

"Welcome to Bay View East High School," he said.

Threading her way through the crowded office, Lake stepped into the hall just as the bell rang. Classroom doors burst open and students rushed into the hallway. It was a lot like Shellerton Forge at bell time, but here everyone seemed to be in a terrible hurry and there were so many more of them, hundreds more. She pressed herself against the wall waiting for them to rush by.

Two blond girls, both wearing large gold hoops in their ears, stopped at a locker.

"Great sweatshirt."

The shirt had the label of a surfboard maker on the front.

"Oh, yeah, thanks. My mom went to California. . . . She got it for me, thanks a lot."

Not only was everybody polite, Lake thought, they were cheerful, too. They smiled all the time, at least girls smiled when they talked together. She wasn't sure yet about the boys.

And, Lake noticed, everything was new: the cars in the student parking lot, the flat-roofed, one-story building itself, certainly everybody's clothes. Like colored clothes in laundry commercials, everything looked bright. Colors were pure and clean, not faded into each other like the clothes she brought with her. She looked down at the shirt she wore. Someone, Andy or Lana probably, had washed it with a load of jeans and now it was blue when it should have been red. That was the trouble when you had clothes that belonged to everyone. Trying not to bump into anybody, she moved down the hall looking for the library and Ms. Appleton's office.

She'd never had an "adviser" before. Ty and Selene and all the others on the farm tried hard *not* to give out advice. It's your life, they said. Think it out. Of course sometimes

144

they couldn't keep their own rule about advice, and even though they wouldn't call it advice, that is what it was. What does an adviser do? Her neck muscles tightened and her jaw ached. Selene would have said she was "uncentered." Trying to relax, she stopped a moment in a quiet little alcove. She breathed in deeply and held it, breathed out slowly with her mouth open.

"*Ommmmm*," she breathed. "*Ah-oh-um.*"

Breathe, hold, release. Again.

But she couldn't make the heavy feelings go away. Even the long braid she'd fixed so carefully this morning seemed heavy, clumsy against her shoulder. She was sure she was the only one in the whole school wearing her hair that way. If only finding her way around this businesslike school and meeting some of the bright, hurried students were as easy as getting into the senior program had been.

The halls were empty now, doors closed. Everyone had moved to the next little slice of the day. She looked at the school schedule Mr. Westcote's secretary had printed out for her. On it time was chopped up into little half-hour slices filled with places to go, rooms to find, books to carry, things to accomplish. She'd never get it all straight. Maybe she'd get a watch, but it would have to be a real watch. A watch with hands and a round dial, round as the earth, to mark the passing hours, not a digital watch blinking out blue tenths of seconds.

On the farm, she thought, time wasn't measured in seconds or even minutes, but in the dinner triangle rung for meals, in sunrises and sunsets, in seasons. A picture of Ty, shading his eyes with his hand, telling the time by the sun's place in the sky, rose in her mind. She would have to keep remembering Ty, hold on to the spirit of Barataria, which was so different from this new world. The vision of Ty's face, animated by the sun, floated away when someone bumped into her, and said, "Oh, excuse me."

Finally there it was. She opened the double glass doors leading into a library filled with more books than she had ever seen in her life. The ceiling soared above her like a banner-draped tent. Off in a little alcove were card catalogs housed in pale gray metal cabinets and straight ahead she saw dark, polished wood tables and even a rug and soft cushions on the floor in a small quiet room. She searched for a sign telling her where the adviser's office might be. Nothing. The only sign visible told her that this was the Multimedia Area. She would have to ask someone, but the room seemed empty.

Then she heard the sound of humming. Someone was humming there in the library. She found him in a corner, a boy curled in a comfortable easy chair in a space labeled Audio Room. He wore headphones and tapped his feet in time to whatever he was listening to. He was small, too small to be a high-school student, she thought, but he was the only one around.

"Would you know. . . ?"

"What. . . ? Oh, hell, wait a sec." He pulled the headphones away, and she could hear the beat of the music.

"The Who," he said. "Really shakes. 'Who Are You?'" he said.

"Me?" she said. "I'm Lake. I'm new and I'm looking . . ."

The boy's mouth fell open.

"That wasn't a question," he said. "It's a song. You know, last year? Top forty? The Who." He nodded yes at her as if he were helping her remember.

"Oh, yeah, sure," she said.

"What are you? A creature from outer. . . ?" he said, still

tapping his foot to the music. She did know The Who, of course. Everybody on the farm had recordings of the rock group from their beginnings in England. But it was mostly old sixties and early seventies stuff, not the most recent albums. And just about the closest thing to The Who the local radio station ever played was Kenny Rogers. She turned to go; she'd find someone else.

"What can I do for you?" the boy said. Was his smile as friendly as it appeared or was he laughing at her?

"I'm looking for a Miss, *Ms.* Appleton's office." She decided to try again.

"New, eh? Senior?"

She shrugged and held out all the printouts and let the papers speak for her.

The boy had dark wavy hair, longer in back than in the front. He kept flipping it in and out of his collar. He wore one gold earring and the thinnest gold watch Lake had ever seen. He was tan, as if he'd been working outside a lot, but somehow Lake knew that wasn't it. Probably he was tan all over, Lake thought. Not like Chad and Kesey whose bodies were white above their rolled-up sleeves and below their shirt collars.

"So, it's your first day? What did you wear that for?" he said, stretching his legs out. He still wasn't very big, even stretched out full length. He looked up at her, curious.

"Wear what?" She looked down at her skirt, knowing exactly what he was looking at and knowing that she had chosen it on purpose. People might as well know right off, she had thought as she dressed this morning, who she was and where she came from. The skirt was red and yellow, one of Selene's creations, mandalas tie-dyed in with beet juice and yarrow weed. She smoothed her hands over the rough fabric. Even though he teased her, for some reason

147

she felt a connection. There was something gentle, easy about him. Maybe he was like Andy, who could tease you, even insult you, but he always did it because he liked you.

"That," he pointed. He was trying not to smile.

"Oh, this old thing?" She held the skirt out with both hands and curtsied.

"It's real, isn't it? Not factory built? Looks like you got it in a museum, you know, like a sixties museum? You get it from a hippie?"

"You could say that." She laughed. It was funny, the tie-dyed skirt here in suburbia. He laughed, too, now.

"Yes," she said. "Actually, you could say that. And now, if the fashion lecture is over, do you know . . ."

"Right behind the stacks, over there." He pointed again. She turned to follow his directions. He stood up to show her the way.

"God," he said. "Wow, she's got a braid, too." And he pulled her hair gently, the way Ty sometimes did.

Ms. Appleton was pleasant, businesslike, and she assigned Lake to honors English, honors history, honors trigonometry, and freshman Spanish. She said that Lake might test out of Spanish later, but that she should speak to her teacher about it. It was his department, she said. When the interview was over, Ms. Appleton sent Lake to sit in on her English class for the last hour of school. Instead Lake went outside to wait for Grand; she couldn't take one more new experience, she thought.

From her place in a pile of golden leaves beneath a sugar maple she could see the kiosk where Grand would stop to pick her up. An hour went by and Lake felt as if she were either invisible or in a spotlight on stage and didn't know the name of the play or her lines. At last the final bell rang and students raced for buses that lined up, grille to

148

bumper, in front of the school. Some ran across the parking lot to jump into their cars. Under the tree at the edge of the lawn she was out of the way of the cars that wheeled out of the parking lot. She was close enough to read the license plates, KOOLISH, EGO-ID, KIDCAR-I. One of the cars drove up and stopped in front of her.

"Hey! Hippie lady! Want a ride?"

It was the boy from the library again.

"My grandmother—she's picking me up. Thanks anyway."

"Come on, come on, get in. She'll be late. I know your grandmother."

"Sure you do."

"No, honest, I do. Grand Thurston. Six-twenty-six Andover Road. She's at a meeting with my mom. I talked to them, honest."

Lake thought she must still look doubtful because he said, "Your grandmother has white hair, she grows anemones, and she's the best carpenter and bricklayer this town ever had. Get in."

He leaned across the seat and opened the door. Kids inside the cars stopped behind him, honked their horns in a cacophony of sound. The horns blended with the loud music from ten radio stations, a different one blaring from each car. The only way to keep everyone from staring at her, honking louder and louder, was to get in the car.

"Get in, get in," the boy yelled. "You're causing a traffic jam.

"Come on, talk to me, hippie lady. You fresh from Woodstock or something?" He turned the corner and drove toward the town square.

"I'm from Kentucky. If you know my grandmother so well, you ought to know that much." She was angry. How had this stranger known more about Grand than she did? She couldn't imagine that the grandmother who sat in her elegant dining room pouring coffee into hand-painted china cups was the same person who could lay bricks or put nails into boards.

"No," he said. "Grand never talks about, you know, her family. All anybody around here can get her to talk about is restoring the old Reynolds house. In fact she won't shut up about it! You know she saved that thing practically by herself."

Lake settled back on the leather seat of the car and watched as the bus station and shops and fast-food places passed by. No one had told her that Grand was a carpenter, that she saved houses. She tried picturing Grand with her hands in cement mud, laying up a line of bricks or caulking a stone basement. She wondered if Selene knew about it.

"Kentucky," the boy said finally. "You're a hillbilly hippie? Wow, that's a real combination. So what is a hillbilly hippie like you doing in this fashion capital of the suburban world?"

"Are you sure?" she said. "Sure that Grand lays brick and all that stuff?"

"Yeah, sure, didn't you know? I'm real sure. Everybody knows about her. You'll see her if you hang around long enough."

Lake watched the sign for Bay Road disappear a block behind them. "Where are we. . . ? I think my street is back the other way," she said.

"Don't worry, we're not going home yet. I told Grand I'd watch out for you. She's never on time, you know, practically lives up at the house," he said as he turned the car into a parallel parking spot. "I'm taking you to the Deli Shoppe. You want to meet and greet, right?"

150

18

"You're awfully quiet," the boy said as he put money in the parking meter. "Don't you want to get to know me and all my friends? Get to know the ropes around here?"

He led her into the delicatessen, which smelled of garlic and chocolate and freshly ground coffee. It was nothing at all like the Piggly Wiggly in Shellerton Forge, which smelled only of red sweeping compound and wet wood, not garlic. In the front of the deli there were red and pale green wine bottles lying in straw on wooden racks. And along each wall were glass cases filled with fat sausages and wheels of yellow cheese instead of the Piggly Wiggly's open shelves holding the ordinary necessities of life, life-sized boxes of corn flakes, rice, and laundry soap. There were so many choices to make here, maybe ten kinds of mustard and even more of pickles, Lake noticed, just as at school or in stores or on TV.

Across the back of the store was a counter and behind it a refrigerator case filled with bowls of potato and bean and fruit salads. Shoppers and kids from school stood in a long line at the counter, waiting to pay for drinks or foil-wrapped sandwiches that they chose from the frosted glass case. The boy took his place in the line.

"You want to find us a booth back there somewhere?" he said. "You want something cold? Or coffee, maybe?"

Lake was glad to move away from the line of people, all talking to the boy, looking past her, staring over her shoulder to talk and laugh with him. They joked, teased each other as if she weren't there, as if she were a life-sized cardboard cutout of a person advertising lime coolers or bread. Finding an empty booth in the back, she sat down, grateful to be out of sight behind the high wooden seats. Now she could look at the people around her. She watched, in a booth nearby, what must have been two mothers and their daughters. They looked like two sets of twins, and except for the careful eyes and the pink masks of makeup the older women wore, they all looked the same age. They dressed alike, too, wore watches as thin as coins, diamond studs in their ears, and had perfect teeth and perfect skin. Nowhere in her new school or here in the deli did she see anyone with the tiny, scabby zits that marked the faces of the runaways who came to the farm sometimes. Nor did she see the pallor, the pastiness of people who had eaten the new macrobiotic diet for too long.

In a few minutes Lake's nameless friend was back carrying three giant paper cups filled with ice and cola on a tray. A small dark girl with cropped black hair stood next to him wearing a blue and gray BVEHS letter sweater. It was so big for her that her hands were hidden inside.

As the boy set their drinks on the table he said, "Lake, meet Caitlin MacLeod. Caitlin, meet Lake Gillespie. You two could be in some classes together, maybe."

Caitlin and the boy slid into the booth opposite Lake and slipped the paper off their straws. Caitlin pushed the

152

sweater sleeves up to her elbows, put her straw to her lips, and blew the paper tube over into the next booth without saying anything about it.

They talked for a moment and then Lake said to Caitlin, "Well, you know my name and I know yours, but what's his?" She jerked her head toward the boy, who concentrated on his drink.

"Boone?" Caitlin nudged him. "Didn't you even tell her your name? You have to excuse him; he's got no manners at all. All he thinks about is being class president. Say you're sorry, Boone." She pushed her shoulder into his.

"Sorry." Boone smiled benignly at Lake.

"That's your real name? As in Daniel Boone?" she said.

"It's Boone," he said. "Short for Boonestoner. But never call me Boonestoner."

"Not if you want to live," Caitlin added.

"What's your first name then?" Lake said.

"That is my first name."

"His last name is Oshevsky. Boonestoner Oshevsky," Caitlin said. "Don't laugh."

Somehow his names didn't fit together. Not like Bascambe Bailey's name and the way it told who he was. "Who, me? Laugh?" Lake said. "You've heard my name. Lake?" She paused. "Go on, ask me," she said. "'Are you one of the *Great* Lakes?' Everybody else asks me that. Why should you be any different?"

As they sipped their drinks Caitlin looked at Lake's schedule, told her who the best teachers were and whom to look out for if she could.

"You're from a commune or something?" Caitlin said. "I thought those places, well, you know, went out with peace signs and Nixon."

"I guess I didn't know peace was out," Lake said.

"I didn't mean . . ."

"It's okay. People make fun of it sometimes. Communes in nineteen seventy-nine? But see my family—my dad—is dead serious, living all that Walden Woods One and Two stuff."

Lake was relieved finally to talk about her other life to someone. Even Grand never asked her anything about Barataria. Maybe Grand's memories of the time Ty and Selene parked their destroyed VW in her front driveway and lived there for two months were so hurtful that she had to protect herself from knowing why it happened.

"Honest," she went on, "I live in a real house with my real parents and we eat real food." She wouldn't tell them yet about the Children's House and how it looked with rainbows colored on the door, shutters painted where there were no shutters. Or about Sun Dog and especially not about Selene.

"I know the food you mean," Caitlin said. "Sunflower seeds and alfalfa sprouts, even apple seeds. You know, whole grains. My parents used to do that, too. They were really weird. They're lawyers now."

"Honest?" She liked this Caitlin and hoped they would be friends.

"They're weirder than ever now." Boone laughed.

"So it's not just you and your mom and dad being farmers." Caitlin said.

"No, we have lots of people. Some come just to study the way my father does things. He knows a lot about organic farming and all that."

"Sounds great."

"It is, but . . ." Lake remembered all the arguments about buying a second tractor and about the hot water they never got around to putting in, how she had wanted a telephone. At Grand's there was no question; the telephone, the dishwasher, and the garbage disposal were just there, to be used and forgotten, and she was sure it was the same at Caitlin's. She didn't dare tell Ty when he called her how quickly she had become accustomed to electric living, to TV, to so many choices. She didn't want to talk about it any longer.

Lake didn't see Boone at school for several days, but he was right; Caitlin was in every one of her classes except freshman Spanish. By hanging out with Caitlin and her friends, by reading the school newspaper and listening to kids in the cafeteria, Lake learned her way around slowly and she was excited by the variety of classes and the big new school. It was special activity sign-up day when Caitlin introduced Lake to girls who played on the soccer team with her. They asked her to come to practice.

"It's not varsity, so you'll make it all right," they said when she told them she had never played. She didn't tell them no one played competitive games on the farm.

"We need size, not experience. You can run, can't you?" they said. "And kick a ball?"

On that same day Boone waved at Lake from across the lunchroom. They stood in the food line together. He pushed his tray along the ledge in front of hers.

"Listen," he said, "you come to play tryouts. They're tomorrow."

"No." She backed up, crashing her tray into the person behind her. Her soup splashed onto her sandwich. "Never. Besides, I said I'd do soccer with Caitlin."

She didn't want him feeling sorry for her. She'd find her own way; she always had. She couldn't act or sing or anything, she told him.

"You can't get out of it. And you don't have to 'act or sing or anything,'" he mimicked her. "You can do lighting or something; do props with me. And by the way, you be sure and tell your grandmother what a good job I'm doing, taking care of you."

The next day Boone practically carried Lake into the little theater where he volunteered her for his prop committee and later stopped at the intramural soccer field to watch her try out for the soccer team.

When she got home from the field that night, tired and elated, the telephone was ringing in the kitchen. It was Tyler on his weekly telephone call to her. When she told him about having play practice or soccer nearly every night, he worried that she couldn't keep up her studies in the big suburban school.

"Honest, Ty, it's okay. Don't forget," she said, "nobody here has to come home and clean the barns or chop weeds out of the cabbages. I can do it. Honest."

Still, with all the extra homework she was assigned by teachers who didn't know her work, Lake was busy the next few weeks, as busy as she'd ever been. She learned her way around the labyrinthine hallways of Bay View, wrote an "A" paper about ethics and values in alternative cultures from 1860 to 1970 in America, and delivered all of Selene's old prom dresses, which Grand let her donate to the theater costume department. It was for a good cause, Grand said.

On another of Ty's calls she told him her Spanish teacher had agreed to let her try Spanish III next semester, and her team had won the intramural soccer tournament. They'd have the play-offs soon. He told her that he had turned the compost heap and shifted the cow to another pasture last week, that Kesey and Chad hadn't enrolled at the Consolidated School, and that he and Free were teaching them as well as they could.

"I got a call from our new agricultural agent," Tyler said. "He wants to talk to me about growing some new kind of exotic vegetables—European varieties, he said, for restaurants. Says it's the newest thing for small farmers."

Lake wondered if that was just one more project like hammocks and mushrooms, but she heard the hope in his voice.

"Have you heard from Selene?" Their voices wove in and out along the phone wires; they'd spoken together.

"I asked you first," Tyler said. "I told her you went up there to Grand's. Told her both my women left me."

"Ty, don't say that," Lake said. "I feel terrible when you . . ."

"Yeah, sure," Ty said, ignoring her comment. "I've heard. Had another card last week. Sounds like she's doing her thing just fine. We're all doing what we need to do to go along life's path, Lakey. Just flow along with it, kid."

"Yeah, that's right," she said.

Sometimes when Ty's calls came late in the evening, Lake couldn't go back upstairs to do her homework somehow. She'd stay downstairs watching late night television on those nights, putting off the time she had to get into Selene's old bed. She let the voices on the TV crowd out the voices of Selene and Ty or Vernelle, or all the others at Barataria, and drown out the ache in her heart. Sometimes after the television screen went dark she sat on the sofa, half-dreaming about Sun Dog, wondering where he might be, maybe painting another house somewhere for another girl? She didn't understand how she could feel relieved and sad at the same time.

But she didn't have to wonder about Selene. Her mother

157

sent postcards almost every day, pictures of the Grand Ole Opry theater or the skyline of downtown Nashville on the front and words crowded together on the back. She wrote that Margo had come through with her first real job. And now she was in a full-time studio group, singing background for soup or car and truck commercials, station breaks, whatever was needed. Now she could work nine to five, she said, and she had weekends off.

"I'm thinking of going back to school," she wrote, and Lake remembered another woman who had left Barataria to go to midwifery school. On her latest card Selene wrote: "I'm listed in some jacket credits now. They used the name Selene, not Eliza, no matter what Margo said, and *in the smallest print imaginable* they put me on the liner notes of a new record cut by some country and western singer you never heard of! But you will someday!

"P.S."—she wrote around the edges of the card—"I'll be cutting a demo soon. I wish you were here to help me decide whether to go pop or rock.

"I love the work, Lake. I miss you."

Grand never got a card and she tried hard not to read Lake's, so Lake left them on the kitchen table every time one came.

19

"Yeeeee-haaa!"

Lake raised up her arms for joy, as if she could grab onto a piece of sky.

"We're born to win!" she shouted.

Even though she hadn't played much because she was inexperienced and even though the game was only an intramural play-off, she was elated, weightless as a bird. Her team beat the junior team, the favorites. She threw herself into the helter-skelter of arms and faces and voices, screaming and cheering with the other girls.

"I never won a game like this; I can't believe it!" she shouted. "It's so great! I love it! Thanks, you guys."

"Did you see that kick she got off?" somebody said. "Lake, it was fabulous!"

"You learn fast!"

"Born to win! Born to win! Born to win!"

Everyone joined in the team cheer and Lake thought her voice was the loudest, the happiest of all. She felt as if she were floating, felt strong and powerful, as though she could do anything. Her face was flushed, she knew, and the blood pounded through her veins. And she didn't care who might see how her smile stretched too wide. She leaped into the air once more.

As the other girls wandered off the field to wait for their mothers to pick them up, Lake found a towel in her duffel to wipe perspiration off her face and bare arms. The sun went behind a cloud, and the air suddenly felt cold against her damp skin. She shivered and pulled on her new sweatshirt, the one with the surfers on it that Grand had bought along with a lot of other new clothes for her. On a zigzagging run she headed across the field toward the park on her way home. Keeping her head down, dancing around imaginary opponents, Lake kicked an imaginary soccer ball toward an imaginary goal. She had gotten halfway across the field with her game when out of the corner of her eye she glimpsed a movement as familiar to her as her own image in a mirror.

Where had the gesture come from? Maybe she had seen movement where there was none. After all, the park was almost empty, only two or three little kids still climbed on the merry-go-round, their mothers talking together at a picnic table, talking in the twilight. Only these few and a lone woman on a swing with her legs stuck out straight in front of her like a child, swinging idly backward, forward. Lake's heart beat hard, once, in her throat, and she felt it lurch inside her chest as if she'd been hit. *No.* She wasn't going to let hope rule her, not again. She stopped, peered more intently into the dusk. No, not in a million years. Selene would never come back to Bay View, not to Grand's territory. Then the woman raised her arm once more in that intimate, gentle gesture. Lake didn't even want to think the words, but when she could breathe again, she let them form inside her mouth. *Selene. It was Selene.*

160

"Lake! When I saw you coming across the park, I knew right away it was you. Did you know it was me?"

"Selene! I can't believe it. You didn't say anything on your last card."

Laughing and crying at the same time, they stood close to the swings. Held in Selene's arms, Lake realized that no one had hugged her that way for a long time. When they pulled apart to look at each other, Lake could smell Selene's perfume on her own skin. Tears filled her eyes as they drew close again.

"You're all . . . different," Lake said.

It was true. Selene was different. She wore makeup on her valentine face now, lipstick and eyeliner, and her dark eyebrows were lighter, plucked into a perfect wing shape. There were silver hoops in her ears, and she wore a black dress with a belt of silver discs as ornate as Sun Dog's. But it was her hair that had changed most: It was wild, curly, the white strands in it colored over. Selene looked young, like a movie star, maybe like someone on the cover of a magazine.

"You haven't changed a bit," Selene said, and fingered the thick braid hanging over Lake's shoulder.

Maybe she hadn't changed on the outside as much as Selene had, but Lake knew she was changed inside and she wanted Selene to notice. When Selene smoothed her hair off her face, Lake's excitement seemed to slide off her shoulders like a silken shirt.

"Come on, I'll walk you home," Lake said. She walked on ahead.

"Wait," Selene said. "Wait up."

Selene hadn't moved.

"Come on, Grand will be home pretty soon." Lake

161

started back toward her mother. "Oh, Mom! It'll be so great . . ."

"No, listen, Lake." Selene held on to her black suitcase with both arms in front of her. "I'm going to go down the hill to the Bay View Inn. I made reservations. We can have dinner and . . ."

"Mom. What a rotten thing to do. Mom, you just get here and. . . ?"

"Wait a minute, Lake. There might be a lot here you don't understand. Things going down you don't know anything about."

"Okay. True. So tell me. Talk."

"You don't remember anything about the last time I was here? I guess you were too little. I . . . she told me"— Selene swallowed hard—"never to come back."

"She didn't mean it," Lake said. "Maybe she had her reasons, Selene. Besides, that was a real long time ago."

"I made the reservation, Lake. I reserved a double—you can spend the night. We'll talk."

Lake thought about how Grand did so many things the way Selene did, how their gardens were alike, how they noticed colors and flowers. Even the work that Grand did on the Reynolds house seemed like something Selene would do—it was just that Grand was looking back and Selene forward. Lake pictured Grand, wearing a pair of faded slacks that were too big for her and a tool apron tied around her waist, showing her around the big old house on Huron Street. Or sitting at the deli uptown with blueprints spread out over the counter showing them to anyone who would look. Why didn't Selene see that?

"You have to come to Grand's. If you don't, it'll only make it worse."

162

"I can't." Selene picked up her bag and started back toward town.

"Go on then. Go on. You're as stubborn as . . . Ty. You two get me so mixed up! If you aren't coming to Grand's right now, I'm not coming to any damn hotel."

Lake stumbled away, her happiness and joy totally gone now. This wasn't at all like those heart-stopping homecomings she'd seen on television. She didn't know whether to be furious or sad. She did know she wouldn't turn around to see whether her mother was following behind her.

"Wait. Damn it, Lake. Wait."

Later in the kitchen at Grand's Selene held her in that old direct gaze everyone did on the farm.

"You okay?" Selene said, bending her head, not letting Lake escape her fierce attention.

"Sure. Yeah. Why not?"

"I mean really *okay*. No bad stuff to tell? No bad scenes?"

"No. I'm fine. Why shouldn't I be? I'm living where you lived, going to the same school you went to, Selene." They both laughed.

Lake forced herself to gaze back into Selene's round eyes, direct and open the way she'd been taught. She didn't know what else to do or say; but now, somehow, their reunion was an interruption instead of a connection. The words of a conversation she overheard in the lunch line at school a few days ago floated through her mind.

"Hell, I haven't seen my mother for over a year," the boy said. He wore three gold chains around his neck. "Then she comes back and points to the sofa and tells me, 'Come

163

on over here and talk to me, son. Let's talk.' Hell, all I
want to do is go to the movies."

"White bread? Nitrites?" Selene asked as she took the
bologna out of the sandwich Lake fixed for her. She ate
the cheese and lettuce standing over the sink, not seated at
the table the way Grand always did. Lake returned the
glass sandwich plate and the cloth napkin to the cupboard.
    "Where's . . . your grandmother?"
    "Historical Society, I guess," Lake said. "She spends a lot
of time there. You should see it—this house, Mom . . ."
    "Sounds like her. Loves the dear dead past."
    Selene spoke in a low voice, stared into the bottom of the
sink where she'd thrown the bologna. She flipped the
switch for the garbage disposal on and off, watching the
meat disappear into the grinder.
    "Mom, she's okay. She's great. I don't see why you can't
see that. Come on, you decided to stay here, now the least
you can . . ."
    "God, Lake, you sure are flat out the way you say things.
It has nothing to do with liking her. She just . . . Oh, nothing ever changes. She's got the coffee pot right there where
it was ten years ago."
    "It's her house."
    "Right." Selene ran her fingers through her long hair,
lifted it, fluffed it out away from her face. "Is she trying to
live your life for you, too?" she said. "I wasn't too crazy
about your coming here, you know. Did I tell you that?"
    "No," Lake said. "You never said." Even on those post-
cards you sent every week, Lake thought, you never asked
me anything about living with Grand.
    "Well, never mind; we still communicate, don't we? We
can get down and get real together. Mainly because I don't

164

expect you to live my life for me. And vice versa. Right?" There was a pause. "Right?"

"Right," Lake said.

It was true. Selene had been her best friend, except for Vernelle. Selene had been her only teacher for so many years and they had shared their deepest philosophies about life and death, birth and love. There was no subject off limits between them, mostly during talks about books Selene assigned as extracurricular reading back then. Her friends marveled. "Are you ever lucky," one of them said. "My mother would never tell me about *that* stuff."

It was true; they had been honest, straight with each other. But now everything had changed and Lake didn't recognize Selene inside or out.

"You'll see." Selene looked out the window through the ivy leaves that had gone brown now in the cold. "You'll see how it is."

20

When Lake took Selene upstairs to put her suitcase into her old room, she heard the side door slam shut. It was Grand; she always slammed the door hard. That was her way, she admitted, of scaring away any intruders who might be lurking inside the house. Sometimes she even brandished one of her hammers when she came into the house.

"Hoo-hoo, I'm home!" she shouted now.

When Selene heard Grand's hello she went toward the open closet with a skirt on a hanger. She faced the back wall and stood with her arms raised, not moving.

"There's Grand," Lake said as if it were big news.

"I heard."

Selene faced the closet wall and Lake thought she might just go all the way in, close the door, and face front in the dark like a child locked in a fairy tale.

"Lake!" Grand was at the bottom of the stairs now.

"God, Lake, aren't you going to answer? Hurry up. She'll be up here and . . ." Selene turned around, her face white, stricken with a look Lake had never seen there before.

"Look, okay. All right. I'll go down and tell her you're here," Lake said. "But you come down right away, Mom. Come right away."

She said it as though she were speaking to a child. A wave of emotion rolled over her. Was it fear, she wondered, fear of a past between her mother and her grandmother that she knew nothing about? Or was it embarrassment at Selene's behavior?

From the bottom of the stairs, Grand looked up at Lake. She still carried the red toolbox the town council had given her last year.

"Look who's here, Grand. It's . . ."

For a moment Lake didn't know what to call her mother. Your daughter? Selene? Eliza? None of those names seemed right. She started down the steps and was halfway down when Selene spoke from behind her.

"Hello, Mother. It's the return of the prodigal freak. You ought to keep your doors locked."

"Good grief, Eliza. Why didn't you let us know you were coming?" Grand said, but then she smiled, a weak indeterminate smile. She put the toolbox on the bottom step and wiped her hands on the front of her jacket. "Good heavens!" she said. "When did you start curling your hair again?"

"I see you painted my room," Selene said, ignoring the question. "It was green, wasn't it, when we were here last?"

"Yes, and before that it was that colonial bouquet, I think. Wasn't that it?"

The two women spoke in blank voices, as if they had no real connection to each other. Selene didn't move toward Grand, and she looked at the carpet as if she'd never seen carpet before. Why was she talking about paint and wallpaper colors when there were so many other things to say? Selene must have read her mind because when she spoke again her voice was more normal, had lost some of its flatness.

"So," she said. "Here we are, three generations. There's Grand at the bottom, Lake in the middle, and me, whoever that might be, looking down at both of them. I wonder if there is any cosmic significance to this arrangement?" she said, and in a gesture Lake had never seen before, buckled and rebuckled the silver belt at her waist.

"When did you get here? Did you have a good trip?" Grand said.

"This afternoon. Actually I took the three-ten train and waited in the park for Lake. She played soccer. That's more than I ever did."

"You were busy with other things. Your music," Grand said, still smiling. "Well, I hope Lake has gotten you settled in the guest room."

"No, actually we'll sleep in the same room. We've done that plenty of times." Selene looked at Lake as if they were conspirators.

"It's not necessary. We have plenty of space." Grand started up the stairs as if she were going to move Selene's suitcase herself. She seemed smaller, older somehow, and lost in the carpenter's overalls that were too big for her.

"Mother. Let it be. We want to be in the same room. We have a lot to catch up on."

After dinner Grand went into her room early "so you two can catch up," she said. Selene and Lake settled down in their shared room. Selene asked Lake all the usual questions about her grades, did she like her teachers, what books was she reading, had she tried to apply for scholarships, all that. Lake's eyes grew heavy. The soccer game had tired her, and after her shower she was even sleepier. She climbed into the small bed.

"You can have your old bed. Tomorrow's Sunday," she said, trying not to yawn. "No school. We'll catch up tomorrow. Okay?"

The next day Selene couldn't seem to settle down; she moved from room to room looking at everything. It was as if by inspecting things Grand had accumulated after Selene left home, by searching for old things in new places, Selene could fill in the last eight years. Maybe, Lake thought, she was looking for traces of her own life there.

"You still file these according to the year, I see," Selene said as she carried four photograph albums into the family room. She lay down on the floor in front of the fire Grand had lighted earlier. A piece of crystal on a chain around her neck rested on the album page and caught the firelight in its prisms.

"Want to take a look at these with me, Lake?"

They spread the leather-covered albums out on the floor next to Grand, who sat with her feet propped on a needle-pointed footstool, knitting with fine, thin yarn. The crackle of the logs, the smell of wood smoke, the warmth on her face reminded Lake of nights around the fire at the farm. The knot in her stomach, the sick feeling, the embarrassment about her mother's behavior began to subside. Things will be better now, she thought, as she turned the pages.

First came the early black-and-white pictures labeled in white ink and pasted onto black pages as thick as felt. There were pictures of Grand and her parents, their cottage on Lake Michigan, Grand sitting on a giant rock at Michigan State, pictures of her wedding to Grandfather.

169

"You come down here, too, Grand," Lake said. "Lie down here and tell us who all these people are."

Lake wanted to understand her mother's family even more than ever. It was as though Selene and Ty and, of course, Lake had been cut adrift from anything in their own past. Maybe that was why Grand was so interested in history. She wanted to understand where she came from, too. Grand put away her knitting and lay down on the floor beside them, her feathery white head next to Selene's.

The second album held yellowish-red Kodacolor pictures of Selene, her face faded, smooth and without delineation. She was Eliza then, wearing plaid jumpers and T-strap shoes, surrounded by Christmas packages or surrounded by aunts and uncles and cousins in front of fourteen different birthday cakes, candles flaming. Seeing her mother amid all these relatives, it occurred to Lake that Selene had traded them for the communal family she invented. *And she left them both,* she thought.

"I wish there were pictures of my whole life like this," Lake said. "Every year of my whole life like chapters, you know, in a story."

"Memories are stored in your brain and heart." Selene tapped Lake's forehead.

That was what they said on the farm, but Lake noticed that Selene turned another page and gazed at the pictures the same way she did at Grand's things. In the next picture Selene wore a peach-colored velvet dress with one bare and creamy shoulder exposed, her hand resting on a music stand. Behind her a black-robed choir watched as someone in a tuxedo handed her a bouquet of roses. Selene turned the page quickly.

"No, wait, I want to see. Where was that taken, Mom?" Lake said.

"That picture," Grand's voice was choked. "That was taken before . . . before your mother gave up everything she worked for . . ."

"*You* worked for, don't you mean?" Selene said. "It was what *you* worked for."

Lake thought maybe those words were the words that had been waiting in her mother's mouth for a long, long time.

"You were so good," Grand said, ". . . so talented. But you had to do it your way. You never listened to anyone else. Not even your father. And do you know what the worst part is, Lake? Now she's back. Beginning all over again. Only in *Nashville!*" Grand spit out the words. "She . . . Your mother won a scholarship," she added.

"Two," Selene said. And then, "Well, there it is, Lake."

She rolled over on her back and stared at the ceiling. "You see before you the major disappointment in your grandmother's life. *Major* disappointment."

Holding on to the wing chair, Grand struggled to her feet and went out of the room. Selene sat up and put her head down on her knees, rocked herself back and forth while Lake, who didn't know what else to do, continued to leaf through the newer albums. There were empty plastic sleeves in them, whole pages left blank as if someone hoped there were pictures somewhere that would tell some ideal story.

Finally Lake found the pictures she longed for, photos of Ty and Selene and a baby, a desert spread out low in the background. All three wore beaded headbands. Strapped to a board hanging from a leafless tree, the baby, with only her square little face showing, looked almost Indian in her round smoothness. Under the picture Grand had written *"Baby Lake at three months—Colorado."* When Lake tried

171

to remember something, anything about this scene, nothing came. It was as if the baby were someone else. She couldn't take her eyes off the picture and caressed it with one finger.

"I look like one of those big-eyed, pale children you see on greeting cards and cheap prints everywhere," Selene said, peering down at the page. "And Ty looks like the Grim Reaper, doesn't he?"

"I hardly knew you then."

It was Grand. She had come back. Clasping the back of the chair, she stood behind it as if she needed protection. She said, "I think we should all try to get along and at least be polite while you're here."

"Oh, right, peace at any price. Isn't that the rule?"

"Mom," Lake said, "let it alone. Can't you?"

Selene put her hand up as if to stop something. "You don't even know what's happening here, do you, Mother? Or that you wanted to take my whole life?"

"And you were so busy reading about yourself in some magazine," Grand said. "Playing your music, listening to the words telling you how awful your life was . . ."

She sounded as if she might cry. "Why, why did you want to learn about who you could be from *strangers*? Never from us? Why did you throw the baby out with the bath water?"

Grand asked those questions as if the answers might save her life. Lake felt the same doors opening into her mother's life she'd seen at the river when Selene read Margo's letter to her, doors she didn't want to look behind. And now it was her grandmother's life, too. Something seemed to break apart in her head.

"Stop! Stop it! I hate this," she said.

"Oh, Lake, I didn't think. I am so sorry," Grand began.

"That's blackmail, Lake," Selene said as if she were still at meeting where everyone knew how to act. "If you have something to add, then say it; but don't cop out and try to stop this."

"Wouldn't you think you could finally see it, wasting all those years and now it's too late," Grand said. "Too late for your music."

"I'm not going to sell out my whole life just so you can say 'I told you so' . . ."

"Nobody is asking you to sell out, whatever that is supposed to mean."

"It means, oh," Selene said. "All I know is, you're not responsible for me. Just worry about yourself."

21

Wearing a trench coat over her black dress, Selene was already in the kitchen when Lake came downstairs to leave for school. Her carry-on bag was on the floor beside her and her hair was full, fluffed out all around her face more than before. With her eyes closed she held a mug of coffee close to her face, breathing its aromas.

"You're up early." Lake took a box of corn flakes from the shelf. "Why so early? Going to go back to your old school with me?"

"Not exactly, no. I'm leaving this morning, Lake. I called a cab." Selene's voice was thick with sleep.

Lake shook her head back and forth.

"You mean you just decided to go?" she said. "Not even say good-bye to anyone?"

"I am saying good-bye. Right now. And I told your grandmother just now." Selene put her cup on the table. "Every time I come here, I let myself be dragged back into all that old stuff, that garbage again. No more!"

"You and Ty, you always say talk it over," Lake said. "Just talk it out with her, Mom." Lake tried to touch Selene's arm, but she drew away.

"Everybody expects something from me. I'm tired,"

174

Selene said. "I feel as if I'm an egg with no calcium in the shell, you know?"

She put her cup on the counter and ran water over the black crumbs from her burnt toast, leaving a reddish brown river in the sink.

"I called a cab to take me to the station. Listen, Lake," she said, "I'll write and I'll see you, honest. I'm not going to lose you."

"Sure. Whatever." Lake shrugged one shoulder and pressed her lips together. And then in one voice they both said, "A person's gotta do what she's gotta do."

"Come on," Selene said when the taxi stopped in front of Grand's house. "I'll give you a ride to school."

"I can walk."

"No, come on. I want to tell you something else."

Inside the cab, which smelled used, like gasoline and cigarette smoke, Selene said one more thing.

"I want to tell you this, Lake. You should know. I'm not going back to Nashville."

Lake didn't want to trust the surge of joy that flooded her body. She flashed on the memory of Selene's old car, how she had chased it up the muddy road, crying in the cold night when Selene left the first time. She could hardly say the next words.

"You're going back?" she breathed. "Back to the farm? Does Ty know? We could both go . . ."

An idea began to form in her mind.

"No, Lake. Not back there. What's different there? Somebody still expects me to be . . . a certain way. No," Selene said. "And you have to stay in school."

"Where then? Where, if not the farm? If not here, then where?" Lake slumped down on the leather seat and watched the meter ticking.

175

Just as the driver steered into the school parking lot, Selene said, "California," with the same broad smile Lake had smiled after her soccer game.

"California! You can't go back there. You're not a freak, a hippie anymore. Why back there?"

"Northern California has a lot of people like me, groups you know, people living as close to their ideals as . . ."

"That's the farm, Mom," Lake said.

"No, this is different. People have good jobs, they make money, they aren't just fringy people like we've always been, living on the margins, barely surviving. No, this is different. They do things for the environment, too. You know, ecology. I can live on a mountain and still . . ." She fingered the glass prism hanging at her neck.

Lake looked at the driver through the rearview mirror, his face blank, sleepy. Why should he care that her life was breaking up again? Selene stopped talking and looked out the car window.

"Here's Bay View, Lake," she said as if she just noticed where they were. "I have to try this. I hope you'll understand. Oh, and I want you to have this."

She handed Lake a package. Wrapped in a blue silk scarf was the handmade silver belt she'd worn that first day on the playground. She kissed Lake and reached across her to open the cab door. When Lake got out, she left the belt on the seat.

Holding hands as they always did, looking married somehow, Boone and Caitlin waited on the front steps near the flagpole for Lake the way they did most mornings. She wondered if they ever stayed the night together.

"Taking a cab to school now, eh?" Boone said. "What happened to toughing it out, all that alternative culture

176

stuff you're so hot about?" he said. "Didn't take you long to sell out."

"Good old Boone," Caitlin said, looking closely at Lake, as though she sensed that Lake was about to cry. "The sensitive, aware man of the seventies, right?"

"Yeah, good old Boone," Lake said when he put his arm around her shoulders.

She didn't want to talk now. There was too much to get used to. Selene was off to some strange place where Lake couldn't picture her. Would there be postcards from a mountaintop in northern California like those she'd gotten from Nashville? Who would Selene be with? There were so many questions.

"That wasn't my taxi," she said finally. "It was my mom's. She left. She had to, you know, go back to work."

"Do you feel terrible? Or are you relieved? Is there the pain of separation?" Boone said, and held a pencil in front of Lake's face as if it were a microphone and he was interviewing her.

"No, neither one. Oh, I don't know." Lake brushed his hand away. "All I know is my mother took off to see the wizard, the wonderful wizard of. . . ? My mother, the rolling stone."

Lake kicked at a piece of gravel, missed.

"Lake, you know what? My mother didn't speak to my grandmother for years." Caitlin put her arm through Lake's. "Not until my mother got through law school. Funny, eh?"

"Now they're like twins," Boone said. "*Her* mother went back to school, too. So hang in there, Lake. I go this way." He turned down a short hall toward his class.

Caitlin went on talking about how her grandmother and mother were so much alike now that the same words came

177

out of their mouths sometimes, but all Lake could think was the way her whole family ran away. Beginning in 1963, Selene ran away from Bay View and then Barataria, and Ty ran from his dead parents and then Noble Justice and the desert.

"I guess it's a family trait," she said to herself. "If you get real about it, I ran away too, didn't I? From Ty and Barataria?"

Lake thought about Tyler and Andy, Lana and Free. With winter approaching they'd be piling up firewood, repairing the tractor and the cars in the dim, cold barn, forking clean straw into the stalls, sitting up late to plan spring planting schedules. Or maybe, maybe they'd all be working in a fast-food place or for the city landscape department. For the first time in a long time, she let her thoughts go back to Sun Dog, too. After watching Caitlin and Boone, who'd made their decision about what love is so early, she was glad she had waited. She would never forget Sun Dog, the sensual mystery of him, she knew, but she wanted more, much more than that, and maybe it was the lessons she'd learned on the farm that had helped her decide. Smiling at the thought, she wondered what it would be like to kiss Boone now, maybe touch the round earring in his ear, feel the smallness of his body close to hers. She closed her eyes.

". . . And so, look, there's no comparison," Caitlin was saying, and Lake was glad she couldn't read her mind.

"Shut up, Caitlin," she said.

"You should go have a swim this morning," Caitlin said. "The girls' team is away. No practice today. Just sneak in. There's never anyone in there this early."

Caitlin was always figuring out ways to solve everybody's problems for them and she knew all the latest theories for mental health. She wanted to be a psychiatrist someday, she told Lake.

"Get some exercise. You're all stressed out," she said.

"I'm okay." Lake touched Caitlin's shoulder. "Thanks," she said. "But I have an early makeup hour. Maybe next time."

They parted at the crossroads of the two main halls and Lake headed for her study hall. Halfway there, she turned around and hurried back to the locker room. She couldn't face the history of the western world now when her own history was so mixed up and weird, she decided. After a quiet swim she'd call Ty from the pay phone in the office, tell him about Selene and ask him . . . The crazy idea that came to her in the taxi this morning whispered to her again, the words stronger than the first time. *Go back. Go back.*

Pulling the heavy door open, she flipped on the locker room light. And then she remembered. There was no telephone on the farm. When Ty called he used the phone at Bascambe Bailey's feed store and mill, their conversations interrupted often by people wanting to say something to Ty. Sometimes all Lake heard through the receiver was the whispery sound of seed corn or wheat whooshing down the chutes into the bins below. She couldn't call him.

She found her suit in her locker and took a quick shower. Entering through an upper door, she saw the pool blue as a jewel below her. Underwater lights glimmered, making ovals of light along the bottom, and the only sound was the blue water fingering at the tile troughs. It was just as Caitlin said, no one was there. As she walked toward the deep end the pool filtering system clicked on and she felt as though she were in a different world, a warm, dim, blue, humming world all alone. No one knew where she was.

179

She was separate, a part of everything and nothing, every possibility seemed to swell before her. On the low diving board she bounced up once and then sliced down into the cold water.

Holding on to her knees, she breathed out, forced herself to stay on the bottom, felt her long braid rise and sway above her. Now she was like Dustin Hoffman at the bottom of his father's swimming pool in *The Graduate*. Maybe she'd stay down there, too, stay until her breath gave out and she had to gulp in water. She tensed, holding her breath.

Who was right? Ty and his patient dream of a perfectible world? Or Selene testing the fit of still another new life? Or Grand preserving the past with muddy hands, holding against a flood of changes? What was right for her? How could she choose? Her chest hurt. There was no more air to ease out of her lungs. Pushing against the bottom of the pool, she propelled herself up through the silver bubbles, wanting to find her family hanging over the edge of the pool waiting to pull her to safety. At the surface she breathed in, devoured air, and there was no one there.

Turning onto her back, she let herself be held in the wide lap of the blue pool. It wasn't like the river. In the river, current carried you along or pushed you under or sometimes took you farther than you wanted to go, crashing you into rocks. There in the river with trout sleeping in submerged roots and the cresses so green and spicy choking the channels, everything seemed out of control.

For some crazy reason, as she swam smoothly up and back, up and back in the lap lane, Lake pictured the automatic pool sweeper sidling like a small crab, crisscrossing, circling the surface of Grand's pool, always working, always efficient. Lake thought about how the long cord attached to

180

the cleaner had proscribed for it the same circles over and over and how Selene upon seeing it must have wanted to dare, dare, double dare herself. Maybe it hadn't been politics and Vietnam and hair and music and blood families, after all, that drove Selene away. Maybe Selene had to leave because her whole life was planned out in places like Bay View, like Grand's, as orderly as a chord of music.

Lifting herself onto the pool deck, she headed for the high diving board, the board that almost disappeared in the steel girders high above her. Because she had learned to swim in rivers where she dived from tree limbs or high banks, she had never been on a high board like this. Her stomach seemed to wrinkle in on itself as she climbed the ladder, clutching the handrails. At the top, remembering Andy's swinging bridge, she walked carefully out to the lip of the board and looked down. In the lighted water below her image wavered in the ripple and sparkle, then bloomed and swelled into many images: Grand, Selene, Tyler, even Sun Dog, Andy and Lana, Boone and Caitlin. She felt for the end of the board, bent her knees, and lifted her arms over her head. In the moment it took to decide to dive she knew that she didn't have to choose one single thing. She'd take something from all of them. She'd choose it all, everything she had been given, she'd use it all.

She pushed herself off the board, arcing into the air.